"Take me to bed," Marisol murmured

Ian didn't need to be told twice. He wrapped her legs around his waist and picked her up. Finding the stairs behind the small kitchen, he carried her up to her room and set her on her bed. Then he drew the sheet up over her, covering her flushed skin.

"Take your clothes off and join me," she said, rolling over to one side and pushing up on her elbow. Then, with a seductive smile, she patted the pillow next to her.

"I can't," Ian replied, sitting next to her and caressing her leg through the fabric. "I'm on duty."

Marisol groaned. "No, no. Call your boss and tell him you won't be in."

Ian chuckled. "I am the boss and I have an example to set. But I'll be back." He bent and kissed her. "You'd better pay that ticket, Miss Arantes, or the next time I see you, I'll have to slap the cuffs on you and ̶ ̶ ̶ ou down to the station."

M ̶ ̶ ̶ ̶ ̶ ̶ ̶ ̶ ̶ ̶ ̶ ̶ ̶ ̶ ̶ ̶ ̶ ̶ d her hand up his ̶ ̶ ̶ ̶ ̶ ̶ ̶ ̶ ̶ ̶ ̶ ̶ ̶ ̶ ̶ oot. He drew in a q ̶ ̶ ̶ ̶ ̶ ̶ ̶ ̶ ̶ ̶ ̶ ̶ ̶ vas betraying just ̶ ̶ ̶ ̶ ̶ ̶ ̶ ̶ ̶ ̶ ̶ ̶ to walk away from her.

But all she said was "Yes, Officer. I'll definitely look forward to that...."

Blaze™

Dear Reader,

What could be more irresistible than a handsome, sexy, Irish-American hero? How about *three* handsome, sexy, Irish-American heroes? The Quinns are back! I've added another branch to the family tree that began with my MIGHTY QUINNS series for the Harlequin Temptation line, and I've turned up the heat.

In this second book of the trilogy, Ian Quinn, small-town police chief, meets a big-city girl who might just be a bit more than he can handle. When Marisol Arantes arrives in town, she stirs up all kinds of trouble with her provocative sculptures and paintings. But Ian is determined to do his duty. Does the policeman's handbook include a section on seduction? Or will Ian have to make up those rules as he goes along?

Enjoy the lives and loves of this irresistible clan. From Marcus last month to Ian this month to Declan next month, there's a Quinn for everyone to love. I enjoy hearing from my readers, so be sure to visit my Web site at www.katehoffmann.com.

Happy reading,

Kate Hoffmann

KATE HOFFMANN
The Mighty Quinns: Ian

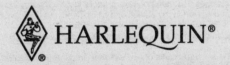

HARLEQUIN®

TORONTO • NEW YORK • LONDON
AMSTERDAM • PARIS • SYDNEY • HAMBURG
STOCKHOLM • ATHENS • TOKYO • MILAN • MADRID
PRAGUE • WARSAW • BUDAPEST • AUCKLAND

ISBN-13: 978-0-373-79289-4
ISBN-10:   0-373-79289-1

THE MIGHTY QUINNS: IAN

www.eHarlequin.com

Printed in U.S.A.

ABOUT THE AUTHOR

The Mighty Quinns: Ian is Kate Hoffmann's forty-ninth story for Harlequin Books. Her first book was published in 1993, and since then she has enjoyed creating sexy heroes that her heroines (and her readers) can't possibly resist. Kate lives in a small town in Wisconsin with her three cats and her computer. She enjoys golfing, genealogy and gardening and also volunteers with music and theater programs for young people in her community. Her favorite place in the whole wide world is her bedroom. But her second-favorite place is Ireland, and it was there that the fairies worked their magic and put the mighty Quinns in her path.

Books by Kate Hoffmann

HARLEQUIN BLAZE
234—SINFULLY SWEET
     "Simply Scrumptious"
279—THE MIGHTY QUINNS: MARCUS

HARLEQUIN TEMPTATION
847—THE MIGHTY QUINNS: CONOR
851—THE MIGHTY QUINNS: DYLAN
855—THE MIGHTY QUINNS: BRENDAN
933—THE MIGHTY QUINNS: LIAM
937—THE MIGHTY QUINNS: BRIAN
941—THE MIGHTY QUINNS: SEAN
963—LEGALLY MINE
988—HOT AND BOTHERED
1017—WARM & WILLING

HARLEQUIN SINGLE TITLES (The Quinns)
REUNITED
THE PROMISE

Prologue

THE HOUSE WAS QUIET except for the ticking of a clock somewhere in the room. Ian Quinn tried to focus on his grandmother's words but his mind continually returned to the clock as he counted the seconds. His younger brothers stood on either side of him, dressed in their Sunday best of well-worn pants and ill-fitting jackets.

Just five years old, Marcus clung to Ian's arm, his face half-hidden from their grandmother's piercing gaze. Declan's rigid posture hid the fear they all felt, cast into this strange place with a woman they'd never met.

"Well," she said, folding her hands over the head of her cane. "I suppose we must make you something to eat."

Ian shook his head. "We had supper on the plane, ma'am. We're not hungry."

She frowned, then slowly rose from the high-backed chair she sat in. Marcus's grip tightened on Ian's arm and he winced. "You may call me Nana Callahan, not ma'am. Though we are strangers, we are family and there is no need to be so formal."

"Yes, Nana Callahan," Ian said obediently. He jabbed Declan in the ribs and his brother nodded his assent, mumbling the words. Marcus simply retreated farther behind Ian's arm.

They'd arrived at the big stone house just a few minutes before, transported from the airport by a black car with leather seats. The flight across the Atlantic Ocean had taken almost seven hours with Ian trying to entertain his younger siblings with cards and books. In truth, he'd been trying just as hard to distract himself from his own fears.

He knew he ought to be thankful for the chance to visit a place as famous as Ireland, thankful that his grandmother had sent the money for the tickets, thankful that the plane hadn't crashed into the ocean and they'd all died. But Ian was having a hard time being thankful for anything right now.

Since his mother's illness had been discovered last fall, the family had been in turmoil. Though Marcus and Declan had been oblivious, Ian had overheard the conversations, mostly about money, insurance, hospital bills, treatments. No matter how hard his father worked, there wasn't enough to make his mother well and support seven children.

Grandmother Callahan had money. A lot of money. But their mother had steadfastly refused to ask her for help. When the annual invitation had come from Ireland for all the Quinn children to visit during summer vacation, Paddy and Emma Quinn were finally forced to accept. But only for the three younger boys.

Ian's other brothers, Rory and Eddie, were old enough to find jobs and his sisters, Mary Grace and

Jane, would help keep the house and care for their mother. Ian had begged to stay, promising his father that he'd find work, but in the end, he was sent away, too. Nine years old just hadn't been old enough.

There had been no hugs or welcoming smiles when they'd arrived at Porter Hall, no assurances that they'd have a good time during their summer vacation. Instead, they'd been hustled inside by their grandmother's driver, Mr. Grady, then escorted into the library by her butler, Mr. Dennick.

"Well, then, how is your mother?"

Ian blinked. He wasn't sure how to answer. "She's fine, ma—I mean, Nana Callahan."

"She's not fine or you wouldn't be here," the old woman snapped. "I know she's sick."

"Yes, ma'am," Ian murmured. The fight between his mother and his grandmother must have been a big one, he mused. His father's parents wrote lovely long letters and sent cards and gifts on their birthdays and at Christmas, at least until Grandma Quinn had died last year. But no one ever talked about Grandma Callahan. Only whispered.

For good reason, Ian thought. He already hated her. She looked down her nose at them as if they were nothing more than trash. And though her house was ten times bigger than the house they'd left behind in South Boston, it was cold and dark and smelled of musty, old things. The sooner the summer was over, the happier he'd be.

"And I suppose your mother told you you've been sent here because they can't afford to keep you anymore."

Ian blinked, her words slicing into him like shards of glass. "That's not true," he shouted. "My ma and da love us. They sent us here because they feel sorry for you. You're old and you're mean and you don't have anyone who gives a shit about you. And I can see why!"

Her only reaction was a slight tilt of her head. "You speak your mind," she said. "I suppose you got that from your father." She paused. "If you speak to me like that again, I will not be afraid to use the strap."

Go ahead, his mind screamed silently. She could beat him until he was black-and-blue and he still wouldn't love her. "We're tired," Ian said. "We'd like to go to bed now."

Her lips pressed into a tight line and she nodded at the butler who stood behind them. "We'll speak more in the morning. Breakfast is at eight. You'll be expected to be dressed by then. Dennick, show them to their rooms."

Ian gave her a cold look before he grabbed his brothers' hands and led them from the room. Why the hell had his parents sent them here? They didn't belong half a world away from the people who loved them. He felt tears pressing at the corners of his eyes and he swallowed them back, refusing to surrender. This wouldn't be a vacation, it would be like spending time in a horrible prison.

"Can we go home now?" Marcus asked as they climbed the stairs.

"Not yet," Ian whispered.

"She's a witch," Declan said. "I swear if she would have hit you, I would have pounded her face."

"Shh!" Ian sent Dec a warning glance, then nodded to the butler, who was waiting for them on the landing. "You'll listen to me now. Da said that I was in charge. I'm to take care of you both. I'll make sure it's all right. I swear."

When they reached the landing, the butler led them into a dimly lit hallway and pointed to the first door. "This would be Master Marcus's room," he said as he opened the door and stepped inside.

"We share a room," Ian said. "At home. The three of us. We'll do that here."

"I don't wanna sleep alone," Marcus said.

The butler's eyebrow arched. "Madam says you are each to have your own room. It would go better for you lads if you minded her." He paused. "You grandmother sleeps in the east wing. She won't disturb you here."

Ian gave the butler a nod, understanding the man's meaning. "It's all right, Marky," Ian said, giving his brother a gentle shove. "Dec and I will just go see our rooms and then we'll come back and tuck you in."

Marcus nodded mutely then slowly walked into the room. He stood right by the door, watching as Dec and Ian followed the butler down the hall, peering around the doorjamb with wide eyes.

Ian had always complained about sharing a room with his younger brothers, but now that he had the chance to have his own room, it didn't seem like such a treat. Each room was dominated by a huge bed with heavy fabric hanging off the posts at the corners. The same fabric hung at the windows, faded by the sun and time.

When Ian reached his room, he walked over to the fireplace and stared at the huge portrait hanging over the mantel. A young boy sat astride a beautiful horse. His face looked familiar, but Ian knew he'd never met the boy.

"That's your grandfather," Dennick explained. "This was his room when he was a lad. You look like him."

Ian glanced over his shoulder. "What happened to him?"

"He died in the war. He was a soldier and was killed by the Germans in France."

"Did you know him?" Ian asked.

Dennick shook his head. "I wasn't yet born when he passed. My father cared for the family back then. He told me Edward Porter was good and kind man."

"Porter? I thought his name was Callahan."

"You'll have to ask your grandmother about the ins and outs of your family's history," Dennick said. "The bath is through that door. You share it with your brother Declan. Clean up after yourselves and we'll get along fine."

The door closed behind Dennick and Ian let out a tightly held breath. Three months. That's how long they were expected to stay. Though Ian hated school, right now he almost wished that it ran over the summer so he and his brothers wouldn't be stuck here.

He glanced up at the painting above the fireplace, his eyes fixing on the boy's face. He had to admit, they did look a lot alike. The three younger Quinns had always favored their mother's more refined features rather than Paddy Quinn's rugged looks.

The boy was dressed in fancy clothes, a blue jacket

and white pants with shiny boots that reached his knees. He held a black stick that looked like a little whip and his eyes appeared to be staring into the distance, as if he hadn't a care in the world.

Ian glanced nervously around the room, then grabbed the chair from the fancy wood desk and dragged it to the fireplace. He climbed up on it and reached for the painting, smoothing his fingertips over the boy's face. He wasn't sure what he'd expected to find, but all at once, there was a connection. It was as if they knew each other, somehow shared the same fears.

His hand trembled and he drew it away, then stumbled down from the chair. His mother used to talk about ghosts and spirits, but he'd never believed in those things. Now, as a chill ran through him, Ian wasn't sure he'd been right.

A soft knock sounded at the door, startling him out of his thoughts. He spun around in time to see Dec and Marcus slip into the room, dressed in their pajamas. Ian smiled and they both rushed over to him.

"I hate it here," Declan said. "We have to call Ma and tell her we want to come home."

"We can't," Ian said. "Ma says we have to be here now and we'll do as she says."

Marcus stared up at Ian, his eyes watery with tears. "Do you think she doesn't want us anymore?" he asked.

Ian shook his head, then took Marcus's hand and pulled him along to the bed. "Nah, don't think that, Marky. She just has to concentrate on getting well. And by the time we go home, she'll be right as rain." He drew back the covers and Marcus hopped up onto the high bed. Declan followed and the two younger boys settled themselves as Ian began to unpack. "It'll be all right," he murmured. "It's only three months. We're tough, we can make it. We'll just pretend we've been taken captive by an evil witch."

"What if she throws us in the oven like in 'Hansel and Gretel'?" Marcus asked.

"She's not really a witch," Dec explained. "She won't hurt us. She can't if we stick together. And if she tries, we'll run away, won't we Ian?"

He turned and nodded, then crossed the room to sit on the end of the bed. He held out his palm. "We stick together, right?" Declan placed his hand on top of Ian's and Marcus followed suit.

"Brothers till the end," Ian said. He glanced at Dec and Marcus and put on a brave smile. In truth, he was just as scared as they were. They were an ocean away from everything they knew and loved, with no way to get back. It might seem an adventure for some kids, but Ian couldn't see it that way. He wouldn't feel truly safe until he was back home in South Boston, in his own room, with Ma and Da just down the hall.

1

IAN SQUINTED against the sun, the glare from the windshield piercing his head like a sharp knife. He'd spent the previous evening with his brothers, drinking far too much beer. It wasn't really a problem since it was Saturday, and as police chief of Bonnett Harbor, he was off the clock. Still, he had to keep an eye on things, at least until he got a cup of coffee and made plans for the rest of his day.

He glanced toward the back of the Mustang, its ragtop neatly folded behind the backseat. A little shade would probably help to get rid of his headache, but riding around with the top up was sacrilege on a beautiful June day like today. He pulled up to the light at Main and Harbor and waited to turn right, knowing it would take precisely thirty-two seconds to change.

"He's doing it again."

Startled, Ian jumped, then glanced over at the elderly woman leaning into the passenger's side of his car. He groaned inwardly and rubbed his forehead. "Mrs. Fibbler. How are you today?"

"You said you'd talk to him," she snapped. "But he's still putting his trash on my side of curb."

The pounding in Ian's head intensified by a factor of ten. "Mrs. Fibbler, technically the land between the sidewalk and the curb isn't yours. It belongs to the town. That's why we can plant trees there without having to ask your permission. I know, you mow the grass there, and by doing that, you believe it's part of your... domain. But I can't stop Mr. Cuddleston from putting his garbage out where he wants. As long as it's on the curb on Tuesday morning then we're all happy."

She frowned, her little flowered straw hat sitting crookedly on her head, giving her a slightly crazed look. "But you promised you'd talk to him."

The light turned green and Ian stuck his hand out and waved the cars behind him ahead. "Did you ever think Mr. Cuddleston does this because he knows you're going to come over and yell at him? I think he likes you, Mrs. Fibbler. And I think, if you were a little nicer to him, you two might..."

She gasped. "Chief Quinn! How dare you think that I would—"

"Become better neighbors," Ian finished. "That's what I was going to say."

She stood up and smoothed her hands over her flowered housedress. "It's only been five years since my Sherman passed on. I'm still in mourning."

Ian sent her a disarming smile, one he'd used so often in his work as police chief. "You're an attractive lady, Mrs. Fibbler. A man like Mr. Cuddleston would have to be blind not to see that." He congratulated himself when a tiny smile crept across her stern expression. It was a wonder how little he used his police training here in Bonnett Harbor and how much he relied on his charm.

"Do you really think he's—" She paused and pressed her palm to her chest, her cheeks coloring with a modest blush. "I—I suppose I could offer an olive branch. Perhaps invite him for dinner?"

"As chief of police, I'd have to say that's a brilliant course of action, Mrs. Fibbler. Brilliant."

The elderly lady bustled off down the sidewalk, a wide smile now beaming from her face, her shopping bag clutched to her chest. She turned back once and gave Ian a little wave and Ian returned the gesture with a weak smile.

"Another damsel in distress rescued from certain danger," he murmured.

When he'd moved back to Bonnett Harbor from Providence two years ago, he'd never expected his social life to take such a hit. It had been easy to date in the city, the available women in endless supply. But here, everyone knew him. If he chose to date someone in town, the entire population knew the details within a day or two. The out-of-town affairs had been satisfying, though short-lived, since his work seemed to consume most of his free time. In the past year, he'd dated three women for a grand total of thirteen weeks.

Hell, he could almost imagine himself as Mr. Cuddleston in a few years, fighting over garbage simply to get a woman's attention. He looked up at the light as it turned red again, then tapped his fingers on the steering wheel, impatient to get his coffee and escape before any other problems arose.

A small sports car pulled up beside him and he looked over at the Triumph Spitfire. Racing green, he mused. Ian had always appreciated vintage cars and this one was one of his favorites. He glanced at the driver, ready to nod his approval, but his breath caught in his throat and suddenly he felt as if he'd been run over by a truck.

Her long dark hair whipped in the breeze, the sun shining on a perfect profile. She tipped her face up and it caught the light just right and Ian continued to hold his breath. She was beautiful. No, more than beautiful. He searched for the appropriate word, but he'd never been much of a poet. *Ravishing* didn't seem to fit. *Stunning* wasn't descriptive enough. He swallowed hard. "Breathtaking," he murmured to himself. It was the best he could do.

She wore a dress made of some fabric that clung to her body like a second skin. Tiny straps held it up, but the neckline dipped low, revealing the tops of perfect breasts. He craned his neck to look more closely, his gaze drifting down to where the dress revealed a long length of leg.

Ian glanced down at his lap, stunned to see he'd become aroused. The woman continued to wait for the light to change. And then, as if she'd felt his eyes upon her, she glanced over at him. They stared at each other for a long, intense moment and the air between them seemed to buzz and crackle, as if a lightning bolt had just struck the space between their cars.

She brushed her hair back from her face, then, slowly, lifted her sunglasses, the smile still twitching at her mouth. Her lips were painted deep red and her eyes were as dark as her hair and ringed with thick lashes. She pursed her lips slightly, as if to blow him a kiss, then let her glasses drop back down.

A moment later she was gone, the car speeding off down Harbor Street. At first, Ian wasn't sure what to do. Then he quickly read the license plate number, committing it to memory. He yanked the steering wheel to the left, determined to give chase and find an excuse for stopping her later. But he popped the clutch too quickly and the Mustang stalled. With a curse, he tried to start the car again. When it finally rumbled to life, she was gone.

As he pulled onto Main Street, Ian grabbed his cell phone and dialed the station. "Sally, I need you to run a plate for me. It's a New York plate. T-B-7-8-4-1?"

"10-4, Boss," Sally said.

"Pull her registration and get me a license, as well. Anything else you can find. I'm on my way in."

"Mr. Cuddleston called this morning. It seems he found his trash cans emptied on his front lawn. He wants you to charge Mrs. Fibbler with trespassing and vandalism."

"I think I've got that problem solved," Ian said. "Just get me that information."

He drove the rest of the way to the station caught up in a fantasy about the woman he'd just seen. He'd always played by the rules and just the thought of pulling her over for no good reason went completely against his grain. But she was different from the girls he usually found attractive, coy blondes with sexy bodies and healthy sexual appetites. Here was a woman who, while equally sexy, could only be called…exotic. His curiosity was piqued and that so rarely happened anymore.

Ian pulled the Mustang into the parking lot behind the station, then hopped out, his thoughts completely occupied with finding her. But as he turned to slam the car door, he stopped short, a dim memory from the previous night floating to the surface of his thoughts.

The celibacy pact. "Oh, hell," he muttered. He shouldn't even be thinking about women, much less chasing one around town! Just last night, he and his brothers had made a pact to swear off women for the next three months. It had been a silly idea and Ian wasn't even sure why he'd agreed to it. He probably wouldn't have if his love life hadn't been pure crap lately. But it was a serious promise, sworn by all three brothers on the gold medallion that had been a holy relic to them since their childhood days in Ireland.

Maybe the plan wasn't such a bad idea. If he stopped looking for the right woman, the right woman might come along. Not that the woman in the green Triumph was the right woman. From the look of her, she didn't belong in Bonnett Harbor—or in his bed.

Besides, he did have his reputation to protect. Though he was a healthy, thirty-one-year-old male, he might as well have been the town minister. Why couldn't the citizens of Bonnett Harbor understand he was just a regular guy who wore a uniform and badge to work? He wasn't always a paragon of integrity and honor. On occasion, he enjoyed being just a tiny bit bad—and sometimes, on occasion, there was a woman involved.

The interior of the police station was cool and quiet as Ian walked inside. The only sounds came from the ring of the phones and the hiss of the air-conditioning. Sally Hughes, the desk clerk, smiled at him as he strolled in.

"Morning, Chief," she said, holding out a blue file folder. "The car is registered to a Marisol Arantes. Address in Manhattan. Pricey neighborhood in SoHo from what I can tell. No criminal record. She doesn't own property in the county, at least not in her name. So what did she do?"

"Nothing," Ian murmured. "So she's not a local?"

Sally shook her head. "Nope. Maybe she was here visiting friends. You want me to dig a little deeper?"

"Thanks," he said, closing the folder. "But there's no need." Ian walked back to his office. Bonnett Harbor was a small town of about 2,500 year-round residents and a full-time police force of eight officers. Nothing much happened beyond a few noisy parties each weekend and the occasional traffic stop. Seeing Marisol Arantes was the most interesting thing that had happened to Ian in at least the past month or two.

He sat down at his desk and opened the folder, pulling out the enlargement of her driver's license photo. Even the DMV had gotten it right. She stared out at him with a sultry look, her lashes lowered, her smile so— He sighed. What would it be like to have a woman like that in his life…in his bed? To have the time to explore her passionate side, to learn every curve and angle of her body, memorize the nuances of her voice and her touch.

"There is one other thing," Sally said, poking her head in the office door.

Ian slammed the folder shut and looked up at her. "It's Saturday. This is my day off, isn't it?"

"You're here, aren't you? I tried to give this to one of the guys on patrol, but they both agreed you ought to handle it since it wasn't an emergency situation and you have a way with people."

"Right," Ian said, standing. He tucked the folder under his arm. "What is it?"

"There's a new tenant over on Bay Street, in that shop with the two little pine trees in front of it. A few members of the biddy brigade have called in to complain there's something obscene displayed in the front window."

"Obscene? Like what?"

"They couldn't bring themselves to say. My guess, a naked breast. They practically died of the vapors when Carmen at the video store put up that poster for that French movie. You know, the one where the lady's dress was half on and half off."

"All right," Ian said. "I'll go check it out, but then I'm done for the day. Understand? Anything else comes in and the boys handle it."

Sally gave him a smart salute as he walked back through the front doors. "You got it, Chief. Enjoy your weekend."

Ian walked back out to his car, then noticed the folder

he still carried in his hand. He opened it up and pulled out the photo once more. There had to be a way to meet this woman again. He shook his head. He'd never been so captivated by a woman before, and never by a perfect stranger.

Ian groaned. Hell, for all he knew, she could be a complete ditz, or a raging harpy, or she could be happily married with three children. Which would probably be for the best considering the most he could manage right now was an affair in mind only. He'd made his brothers a promise, sworn on the gold charm, and he had two weeks' pay riding on three months of complete celibacy.

He leaned against the Mustang and studied her features for a moment longer, wondering just what it was that made her so attractive. Finally, he slipped into the car and tossed the folder on the passenger seat. He'd never see her again, so what was the point in thinking about her?

Ian put the car into gear and steered out of the parking lot, turning toward Bay Street. Running parallel to Main Street, Bay had a small collection of shops and boutiques as well as a few art galleries. More and more of the buildings were being renovated and rented out to businesses that appealed to the summer crowd. Before long, Ian expected that Bonnett Harbor would be second only to nearby Newport as a tourist destination.

He parked the car in the first available spot, then got out, not bothering with the meter. Ian scanned the windows up and down the street as he walked, searching for something that might be considered "obscene." A moment later, he came to a stop in front of the two small pine trees. Three sculptures stood in the plate glass display window, each perched on a stark white pedestal. And they all featured the naked male form between the waist and the thighs.

The sculptures, though fashioned out of clay, looked disturbingly lifelike. They weren't technically obscene, just very detailed and realistic. And fairly well endowed. He walked to the door and peered inside through blinds half-shut. The interior was in disarray, as if the new tenant was just moving in. Paintings were leaned up against the walls and other sculptures sat on pedestals, covered in bubble wrap. Ian tried the door and was surprised when it opened.

As he walked inside the cool interior, sounds of an opera aria echoed through the shop, the soprano voice sweet and soothing. "Hello," he called. "Anyone here?"

A few seconds later, he heard footsteps on the polished hardwood floors. And then, as if by magic, she appeared. The woman in the green Triumph. He frantically tried to recall her name. Marisol…Marisol Arantes. But then, he wasn't supposed to know her name. Ian sucked in a quick breath as he watched her approach, her thin silk dress molding to her slender body as she walked.

"Can I—" She paused. "It's you," she said. "From the stoplight."

Ian nodded and pulled his badge from his jeans pocket. She remembered him, as well. That was a good sign. "Ian Quinn," he said. "I'm chief of police here in Bonnett Harbor. And you're…"

"Marisol," she replied, her whiskey-tinged voice sending a shiver down his spine. "Marisol Arantes."

She didn't offer her hand and Ian found himself disappointed. Her fingers were long and slender, tipped by short, unpolished nails. He noticed a streak of blue paint just below her wrist and fixed on it for a long while.

She cleared her throat, jerking him out of a study of her left forearm. "Is there something I can do for you? I believe I have all of my permits in order, don't I?"

He met her gaze. "I've been asked to come here to discuss the pe—" Ian paused. "The…art in your front window."

She stared at him in a very disconcerting way and Ian shifted, unable to read her expression. Women usually found him charming, but he sensed that Marisol Arantes was used to getting more from her men than a winning smile. He was seriously out of his league here.

"You've been asked?" She took a step toward him, observing him shrewdly, then slowly circled him, her eyes raking his body as she moved. "Do you always do what people ask of you, Mr. Quinn?"

"Miss Arantes, this is a very small town. And though your sculptures and paintings might be…fascinating to big city folks, people around here find them a little unnerving."

"Do you find them unnerving?"

He chuckled softly as she circled back in front of him. "Do you always ask so many questions?" he countered.

She smiled. "I'm curious. What do you think of my art?"

"I don't know much about art," Ian admitted, taking in the paintings and sculptures scattered about. She was standing so close he could smell her perfume, even feel the heat from her body. "I know the *Mona Lisa* is good and Elvis on velvet is bad, but beyond that, I can't offer an opinion."

"Ah, but it's not an opinion I seek," she said, her voice taking on a seductive tone. "But your reaction." She placed her palm in the middle of his chest. "How you feel right now? Physically? Emotionally?"

If she wanted to know, he could tell her. His heart was pounding so hard he could hear it in his head. His fingers itched to reach out and touch her, to skim his palms over her arms, to circle her waist and pull her against him. And he was afraid to look down, afraid that he was having the same reaction to her that he'd had in the car. Beyond that, he wondered just what, if anything, she was wearing under the flimsy dress.

If she knew the effect her touch was having on his body, she didn't show it. Ian tried to moderate his breathing, tried to appear calm. But he was finding it nearly impossible now that the warmth of her hand had seeped into his skin. He scanned her features, taking in the heart-shaped face and the lush lips, the wide eyes and the thick dark hair.

If he just leaned forward a bit, if she gave him the tiniest hint of interest, he'd be forced to kiss her. Once he did that, they could put all this small talk behind them and get down to the business of this crazy attraction between them. There was an attraction, wasn't there? He wasn't reading the signs wrong.

"Well? Are you feeling anything?" she asked.

Ian drew a deep breath and cleared his throat, trying to focus his thoughts. "Yes," he murmured, his voice cracking. Confusion, exhilaration, insecurity. He'd made love to his fair share of women, but suddenly, he felt like a complete rookie. If he could barely talk to her, then how the hell did he expect to seduce her?

"They make me feel…inadequate," he said as he stepped away. He wandered over to another sculpture. Ian studied it for a moment, then winced, the instinct to avert his eyes a bit too ingrained in his psyche.

"I know," she said with a wicked smile. "Sometimes it's difficult for men to appreciate my work at first. But you have to get over that whole urinal thing."

He gasped. "What thing?"

"You need to see the cock as a work of art," she said. "Not as some kind of yardstick you all measure yourself against."

Her use of a nonmedical term for the male anatomy only added to the desire racing through his body. The word sounded so tantalizing coming from her lips. "A yardstick would be overkill for most men." Ian pointed to the sculpture. "This isn't all there is to the male body."

"But it's the most important part," she said, her tone becoming passionate. "It all comes to this, don't you agree? Life, death, love, hate, fidelity, betrayal. This is the essence of what it is to be a man. This is what drives you, what makes you who you are, right?"

"No," Ian said. "Well, not entirely. I mean, not all the time. Though most women would like to believe we think with our…penises, it's not true. We do use our brains on occasion."

What the hell was he doing, discussing penises with this woman? How had they managed to take a very promising meeting and turn it into some psychological examination of men's libidos?

Marisol reached out and ran her hand over the sculpture, her fingers caressing the sculpted penis as if it were real. Ian's reaction was immediate and intense, the blood rushing to his crotch. It didn't take much imagination to see how she might touch warm, living flesh. *His* warm, living flesh. He could almost feel it now.

Ian turned and walked away again, afraid his reaction would become increasingly apparent. As he crossed the gallery to a large painting on the wall, Ian tugged at his T-shirt, until it covered his groin. Everywhere he turned there were penises, in all different sizes and colors, some attached to men's bodies, others just floating in space. "Why are you so fascinated by this subject?" He glanced over his shoulder and watched her approach.

"Fascinated, curious, mystified," she said, her eyes fixed on the painting. "Sometimes bothered."

"Perhaps a bit obsessed?" Ian added.

"It's a curiosity. I don't have one, so I'm left to wonder how it all works, how it feels, the power that this thing has over a man's psyche. I think by painting them, I'm searching for understanding."

"Did one of these units—" He paused. "Did one of these guys do you wrong?"

She tipped her head to the side as she stared at the painting, her pretty face taking on a distant look. "I suppose you could say that. In the end, it came down to this." She shrugged. "He found someone he desired more."

"I'm sorry," Ian said.

"There is nothing to be sorry for. Why would I want a man who didn't want me?" She shook herself out of her daydream and glanced over at him. "Well, I've revealed all my secrets to you, now you need to tell me one of yours."

"I don't have any secrets," Ian said.

"And I don't believe you," Marisol replied. "But if you're too afraid to tell me, I'll understand. It's probably your job that makes you so uptight? The badge, the uniform, all the laws to follow. It's probably why all of this makes you so uneasy."

Ian bristled at her comments. What was wrong with being a stand-up guy? People trusted him, they looked to him to know what was fair and right. He'd learned early to take responsibility, and though it may be oppressive at times, that didn't mean he'd turned into Dudley Do-Right. "Listen, I understand this subject is important to you. But do you have any other pieces you could display in the window? Maybe a nice cat or a bowl of fruit? A horse?"

She stood by his side, shaking her head. An impulse skittered through him and he fought it back. He wanted to kiss the curve of her neck and he wondered how the skin would feel against his lips. But rather than give in to his impulses, he would take care of business and get out of this shop.

"This is my work now," she said, her voice calm and even. "If people have a problem with it, then they don't have to look. An artist has every right to express herself in any way she chooses, don't you think?"

Did that go for the man standing beside the artist? What if he chose to express himself by yanking her into his arms and kissing her? Or by brushing the straps of her dress off her shoulders and letting it slip to the floor? Or by laying her naked body across one of the padded benches and losing himself inside her? Surely if she expected him to accept her personal expression, she would be willing to accept his.

"There's no law against it," Ian admitted. "After all, it is free speech. But I can't say it won't cause problems. If I don't do something about it, then the village board probably will."

"Good. Then you can tell these people we spoke and that I won't be taking my sculptures out of the window." Marisol grabbed his arm and walked Ian to the door. "I should get back to work. My opening is in another few weeks and I have a lot to do. It was a pleasure, Mr. Quinn." She met his gaze and Ian saw a flicker of desire there, a subtle shift in her expression that revealed more than words could say.

"You wanted to know how all this makes me feel?" Ian asked.

She nodded.

Ian drew a deep breath, then slipped his arm around her waist and pulled her against him. A moment later, his mouth found hers, and he kissed her, slowly and deliberately, mustering every ounce of skill he'd ever possessed. When he finally drew back, he watched her eyes flutter open, then grow wide with shock.

"I—I see," she murmured.

"I'm glad," he said. He turned and opened the door, then stepped out onto the sidewalk. An instant later, the lock clicked behind him.

Ian walked back down the street to his car, satisfaction slowly growing inside him. He'd handled that quite well. Though it wasn't the most auspicious beginning, it was a beginning. But as he got closer to his car, the reality of what he'd just done began to sink in.

"What the hell was I thinking?" he muttered. He'd been at her gallery in an official capacity and he'd forgotten every rule of law enforcement because of what was going on in his jeans.

Maybe Marisol Arantes was right. Maybe it was all about a guy's penis—and the woman who controlled it. Well, at least he'd have a chance to prove her wrong. In fact, he hoped like hell she'd keep her naughty little sculptures in the window. Now that the object of his sexual obsession was living in Bonnett Harbor, he'd have plenty of opportunities to see her again.

"YOU REALLY SHOULD be getting back, Papi. It's a long drive into the city and it's late." Marisol watched as her father wandered around the gallery, stopping in front of each of her paintings, examining them with a discerning eye.

She'd never been bothered by the critics and their

opinions of her work. But when it came to her father, his was the approval she sought. In truth, the reason she'd first grown interested in painting was because of him. He'd had aspirations to become a famous artist at one time, but the public had not been kind to Hector Arantes. Though he'd had some success in Europe, he'd hoped for even more in the U.S. So he'd brought his wife and his five-year-old daughter from their home near Lisbon to New York. And from the very moment they'd landed, things had begun to go wrong.

The critics had been brutal and her father, desperate to provide a living for his family, had fallen in with some unscrupulous men, swindlers who had offered him a great deal of money to take part in their schemes.

Though he hadn't possessed a talent for his own work, Hector Arantes had an uncanny ability to copy the work of other artists. She hadn't been aware of it at the time, but her father had become notorious for forging little-known works by well-known artists to feed a market in the Far East. When he'd been caught seventeen years ago, it had cost him a prison sentence. He'd been gone from the time Marisol had been nine until she was nearly nineteen. She and her mother, a former Russian ballerina, had struggled, living in a tiny flat in SoHo while her mother taught children's classes at a small community center.

For all those years, Marisol refused to put him out of her life and when her own art began to gain recognition, she'd refused to heed the advice of her friends and change her last name. The Arantes name had become infamous in the art world, for all the wrong reasons. Still, it was her name, a name she wore proudly.

"Maybe you should start to paint again," Marisol said. "The market has changed and your work might be accepted now."

Hector shook his head. "No, it is too late for me to make a career. I have my life in the city, my students, a few friends. I paint murals for rich people's houses and they appreciate my work. I am the poor man's Michelangelo. I want nothing more."

Her father was a proud man, even after he'd been beaten down by life. Marisol had tried to make his life more comfortable, but he'd refused all help. And her mother had put him out of her life the day he'd been convicted. Marisol had been left to keep the shreds of her family together.

"So what do you think?" Marisol said. "It's a nice space, no?"

"I don't understand why you moved out of the city, Mari. What is out here but a bunch of bourgeois suburbanites who buy their art to match their sofas?"

That's what Marisol had thought when one of her patrons had first offered her the chance to have her own gallery. But after yesterday's encounter with the village police chief, she'd been forced to alter her opinion of Bonnett Harbor. A shiver prickled her skin and Marisol rubbed her arms, making a note to adjust the air-conditioning in the gallery. But even she could admit that her reaction had nothing to do with the room temperature.

Ian Quinn had been invading her thoughts from the

very first moment she'd seen him yesterday. How many times had she sat at a stoplight and glanced over to look at the driver beside her? Hundreds, probably thousands. And how many times had that driver been a man who'd been the embodiment of every fantasy man she'd ever had? Only once.

After she'd driven off, Marisol had been certain he would follow her, certain that he'd felt the same intense attraction. And when he hadn't, she'd accepted the fact that her imagination had been playing tricks on her. Perhaps the stress of opening the gallery and working until all hours of the night had made her delusional.

But after his visit yesterday morning, Marisol knew the attraction was very mutual. In truth, it was more than just an ordinary attraction. When he was near, her body seemed to tingle with anticipation, as if indescribable pleasures were just a heartbeat away.

Marisol had always been quite comfortable with her sexuality. Through her art, she'd made a careful study of the male anatomy, but she'd also enjoyed the pleasures of a man's body whenever the urge struck her. She'd had lovers in the past, some of them for a night, others for a much longer time. But she'd kept to one philosophy—sexual attraction, especially one as strong as she felt for Ian Quinn—deserved to be satisfied.

"Mari? You're not listening."

She sent her father an apologetic smile. "I'm sorry. I have so much on my mind. What were you saying?"

"I was asking what this place has that the city doesn't."

Besides Ian Quinn? "Well, Papi, right across the bay

is Newport. I have several clients who summer there and they've promised to introduce me to their friends. And Sascha is still showing my work at her gallery in SoHo. I'm just expanding my clientele. Besides, it's quiet here. No distractions."

No David, she thought to herself. He'd been the sole reason she'd had to escape New York. What had begun as a wildly passionate affair had ended horribly. They'd moved in the same social and business circles so it had been nearly impossible to avoid running into him—and his new paramour, a twenty-one-year-old Brazilian model, lithe and leggy, and completely brainless.

He was supposed to have been the one, the man she could spend the rest of her life with, a passion that would never die. David Barnett was an art dealer and their careers had meshed perfectly, as perfectly as their bodies and their hearts had—or so she'd thought. She'd come home one day and found the Brazilian naked, in their bed, with David. And just as quickly as it had begun, it was over.

Now, as Marisol looked back on it, she wasn't sure whether she'd loved David at all. Maybe she'd just been swept away by the need, by the way he touched her body and piqued her desire. Perhaps she'd confused those feelings with something deeper and more lasting.

She wouldn't make the same mistake twice. She'd learn to separate desire from emotion. And what better way than to test herself on Ian Quinn? He had almost everything she could possibly want in a lover—he was tall and dark, sexy and charming. It remained to be seen whether the sex would measure up, but that question could be quickly answered the next time they met.

"You're right," Hector said. "I should get back. It is a long drive."

They silently walked to the door, then stepped out of the cool interior of the gallery into the humid night. Marisol threw her arms around her father's neck and kissed him on both cheeks. "Drive safely, Papi. And call me when you get back. I'll be working all night."

She stood on the sidewalk and waved as her father drove off in his battered old car. It wasn't until she turned to go back inside that she noticed the shadowy figure standing beneath a nearby streetlamp. Her Manhattan instincts kicked in and she hurried back to the door, ready to step inside and lock it behind her. But then she recognized the tall, lean form and the perfect profile.

"Are you spying on me, Mr. Quinn?" she asked, hitching her hands on her waist.

"I was just out for a walk," Ian replied as he approached. "I couldn't sleep." He nodded toward the street. "So, you had a date?"

"Is this part of your job? To know everybody's business in this town?"

"I'm paid to keep an eye on things," he said, his gaze lazily raking her body.

Marisol felt a delicious shiver rush over her. She knew that look, that simple way a man had of acknowledging sexual need. Her immediate instinct was to rebuff the advance, to protect herself from the hurt she'd suffered at David's hands. But she was most curious to see where this all might lead. Perhaps sex with Ian Quinn would be exactly what she needed to forget past mistakes. "On me?"

He nodded. "Now that you live here, yes."

"Would you like to come inside?" she asked with a coy smile. "I can offer you a drink. It might help you sleep." He paused for a long moment and she thought he might refuse. The invitation was so obviously transparent.

"All right," Ian finally said. He followed her inside, then walked with her to the back of the gallery. A modern couch, upholstered in a pale green fabric was set against the back wall. Two armchairs that Marisol had purchased in New York were positioned across from it.

Ian sprawled on the couch, resting his arms across the back, his long legs stretched out in front of him. "So this guy you were kissing. Is he someone you've been seeing for a long time?"

"You might say that," she replied. He was awfully nosy. Was he simply doing his duty as police chief or was he already jealous? "He's my father. He drove out from the city to have dinner with me and to see the gallery."

"It's late for him to drive back."

"We're both night owls," she said. "And he hates the traffic so he does his best to avoid it." She wandered back to the small kitchenette and grabbed a glass, then retrieved a bottle of Scotch. "Is this all right?"

Ian nodded and Marisol poured him a glass, then sat down next to him on the sofa. "Why are you really here, Mr. Quinn?"

"I told you, I couldn't sleep."

Marisol took a sip of his whiskey, then handed him the glass. He really was stunningly attractive. His hair was dark, nearly black, but his eyes were a deep blue, a color that was a mix of azure and cobalt. She stared into those eyes, trying to memorize the exact hue so she might replicate it with her paints later.

His gaze dropped to her mouth and Marisol watched as he contemplated kissing her. But when he looked up again, she found herself overwhelmed by the prospect. One kiss and it would be all over between them. Choices she had now would be lost forever. She already knew the effect his mouth had on her and couldn't imagine what his touch might do.

She slowly rose up from the sofa and walked over to a ladder she'd set beneath a row of track lights. Her breath was coming in short little gasps and she felt light-headed. Was it exhaustion or had he done this to her? Grabbing a lightbulb from the case she'd purchased, Marisol slowly climbed the ladder. When she looked over at him, he was still watching her with a lazy fascination.

So much for playing it cool. She might as well write Seduce Me in big letters across her forehead. Though he seemed to hide his interest behind a mask of indifference, Marisol knew the real reason he'd come to her. It was evident in the predatory way his gaze followed her.

"I have so much to do," she said.

Ian slowly stood, then set his glass down on the coffee table. When he reached the ladder, he braced his hands on either side of her legs, trapping her where she stood. "Why don't you let me do that?" he said. An instant later, his lips touched the soft skin behind her knee. It was such a silly spot to kiss, but the warmth of his mouth sent a thrill to her very core.

She closed her eyes as he lifted her skirt, moving higher and higher with his mouth, the trail of kisses damp on the back of her thigh. On shaky legs, Marisol slowly descended the ladder, the bulb still clutched in her hand.

He didn't step away, and as she continued down, she found herself brushing up against his body, her backside coming into contact with his crotch. It was as if he were challenging her, tempting her to react. She slowly turned, leaning back against the ladder for support.

"I'm trying to figure out why I want to kiss you so much," he murmured, leaning closer.

"Is it necessary to have a reason?" she asked.

"Don't you think it might be dangerous not to?"

"Curiosity," she said, running her fingers through the hair at his temple. "There's a good reason."

"All right," he said. "Curiosity, it is."

Closing her eyes, she parted her lips and waited, certain it would be wonderful. The moment his lips touched hers, a wave of pleasure washed over her body. His hands skimmed along her torso, then caressed the curves of her hips and waist. It had been six months since she'd felt this desire, since she'd been touched so intimately by a man. As his tongue dipped into her mouth, Marisol's knees went weak. What Ian Quinn knew about kissing was a lot more than most men knew, more than any man she'd ever kissed knew.

He was gentle at first and then as she surrendered, his

hands began to explore with greater intent. The silk dress was a feeble barrier to his touch, the warmth of his palms penetrating the fabric to leave a brand on her skin.

He drew back, then cupped her face in his hands, running his thumb along her jaw as he stared into her eyes. Marisol held her breath and waited. His gaze skimmed over her face, lingering on her lips, wet from his mouth. With each heartbeat that passed, she wanted it more, just one intense and intimate connection to ignite the spark between them.

"Remember how you said I was afraid to break the rules?" he asked.

Marisol opened her mouth to speak, but the answer died in her throat. Instead, she just nodded.

"Going any further with this would break a lot of rules."

"They're not our rules, are they?" Marisol asked. As far as she was concerned, there were no rules when it came to the desire between a man and a woman. They just needed to follow their instincts and let their needs guide them.

His mouth came down on hers again and this time the kiss was desperate and deep. Marisol wrapped her arms around his neck and furrowed her fingers through his hair, lost in the whiskey taste of him. Every tiny movement of his lips and his tongue was meant to tantalize and she couldn't help but respond.

He grabbed her backside and lifted her up, wrapping her legs around his waist. Marisol let the lightbulb drop to the floor and it shattered behind him. But Ian didn't react, so intent on ravaging her mouth.

He pressed her back against a pillar and then slid his hands along the length of her thighs, from her knees to her hips and then back again. The fabric of her skirt caught between them and Marisol tugged at it until it gathered around her waist.

The touch of his hands on her naked skin was almost more than she could bear. And yet, it wasn't enough. She wanted to rid herself of the dress, to open her body to his caress and revel in the sensations that his touch elicited.

She was supposed to be invulnerable to a man's charms, especially after what David had done. But all the promises she'd made to herself had simply vanished the moment Ian had kissed her. She needed to feel the rush of anticipation, the flood of desire and whirl of passion again. It would fill her up with heat and energy and she'd feel alive.

Marisol let her legs relax and slowly, she regained her feet. She reached between them and began to work at his belt. He offered no resistance and instead, bunched the fabric of her skirt in his fists, drawing it back up around her waist.

He nuzzled her neck, then whispered into her ear, "What are we doing?"

"I don't know," Marisol said. "But it feels good."

"Mmm." The sound was a low growl in his throat as her fingers moved to the zipper on his jeans. His hips pressed against her hand and she could feel the hard ridge of his erection between them. This was all happening so fast, but she couldn't seem to stop herself.

His hand smoothed along the inside of her thigh,

then back to her hip, brushing against the spot between her legs. The contact brought a moan to her throat and she tugged at the waistband of his jeans, exposing the boxers beneath. Suddenly, it all became so frantic and desperate, as if they were racing against some clock that might unexpectedly signal a return to reality.

Clothes were pushed aside, skin exposed, and Marisol wrapped her fingers around him and slowly began to stroke his stiff shaft. In turn, Ian tugged her thong down and slipped his hand between her legs, his fingers teasing at the soft folds of her sex. She moaned, but then he froze.

"Shit," Ian muttered, collapsing against her. "I don't have a condom."

"You're a cop," she said. "Aren't you supposed to be prepared?"

"That's the Boy Scouts." He buried his face in the curve of her neck. "I had one, but I took it out of my wallet."

"Why would you do such a thing?" Marisol whispered, her fingers still gently stroking him.

"I just didn't expect to—" He sighed. "It's a long story."

And then, the reality alarm rang. She didn't expect this, either, this wild and irresistible attraction, this dangerous need to feel him buried inside her. "We can't do this," she said with a shaky voice. "I—I mean, we can, but we probably shouldn't."

He stepped back and nodded. "I usually don't…I mean, this isn't the way I…" He raked his hand through his hair, shaking his head. "I don't know what happened here. I'm sorry, but I—"

"No," she said, holding out her hand to stop his apology. "It was me. All of these things have been building up and I just needed—"

"It was me," he insisted.

Marisol pressed her finger to his lips. "It was both of us. So there's no need for apologies."

He winced as he pushed himself back into his boxers, then zipped his jeans. Marisol smoothed her skirt down along her legs, pulled the straps back up on her shoulders, suddenly embarrassed that she'd let this all go so far. What had she been thinking? She hadn't, that was the problem. Using Ian Quinn's body to put David out of her mind wasn't the smartest move in the world. She'd been desperate to prove she could enjoy sex without an emotional attachment. But the feelings running through her were proof that there was something more than just simple lust at work here.

"I'm going to go now," Ian said.

"All right." She watched as he walked to the door, a maelstrom of indecision swirling inside her. She didn't want him to leave. She wanted him to strip off his clothes and make love to her, to ease this ache that had taken up residence deep inside her. And she wanted to fall asleep in his arms, wrapped in his embrace, and wake up in the middle of the night to do it all over again. "Good night," she called, a bit too cheerfully.

He reached for the door, then froze. Slowly, he turned. In a few long strides he was back to her, sweeping her into his arms and kissing her again. It came so quickly, she barely had time to react and then it was over, her mouth damp with the taste of him, her lips bruised.

He pressed his forehead to hers and smiled. "This is going to happen between us," he said. "It's just a matter of time. You do know that, don't you?"

"Yes," she replied. "I know."

He stole another kiss, then walked back to the door. "I'll be seeing you, Miss Arantes." He grinned, then disappeared into the night, the door swinging shut behind him.

Marisol drew a deep breath and closed her eyes. Her thoughts were filled with images and sensations, swirling together until she couldn't think straight. His mouth on her throat, her fingers wrapped around his cock and the powerful current that had raced between them.

She'd always been comfortable with her desires and her ability to satisfy them when necessary. But before she fell into bed with Ian Quinn, she'd better be ready to handle what came after.

2

"I THINK WE GOT the raw end of the deal," Declan said.

Ian stared into his coffee, waiting for the caffeine to kick in. He hadn't slept at all last night. Instead, he'd stared at the ceiling, trying to figure out what the hell had happened between him and Marisol Arantes. It was as if the moment he met her, every rational thought in his head had just decided to take a vacation. She took his breath away, and his ability to control his desires.

Ian took a sip of his coffee, looking over the rim at his younger brother. "I know. It was a sucker bet. Marcus knew he'd be the one to win. He's stuck all alone on that boat for the summer, anchored offshore. He might as well be living in a monastery in Tibet." He set the coffee down and poured an extra measure of sugar into the cup, then slowly stirred it. "Maybe we ought to give up right now and pay him the money. Why torture ourselves?"

"No way," Dec said. "We can't let him win. We just have to last three months, until the end of the summer. If we manage for that long, then at least we'll break even."

"Why did we agree to this again?" Ian asked.

"We're supposed to take the time to learn a little

more about women," Dec said. "And maybe a little bit about ourselves. A guy really doesn't know himself until he faces adversity, right?"

"We're not crossing the North Pole here," Ian said. "Or climbing Mount Everest. You make it sound like celibacy is going to be life-threatening. There are a lot of guys in this world who go three months without having sex." Hell, Ian had gone five months, until last night. Though, technically, last night hadn't been full-on sex, the fantasy had been real enough when he'd found relief in the privacy of his own bedroom.

"Not by choice," Dec said.

Ian had to give him that. He'd never in his life made a conscious decision to avoid women. In turn, he had always seemed to be surrounded by attractive ladies—until he moved back to Bonnett Harbor two years ago. Now, a day after he had vowed to give them up, Marisol Arantes waltzed into his life with her dark eyes and her kissable mouth and a body that begged to be touched.

The squawk of Ian's radio interrupted his thoughts and he grabbed it from the clip on his shoulder and pushed the button. "Quinn," he said.

"We've got a traffic problem on Bay Street," Sally said. "Delaney is over there and he says he needs backup. Wilson is tied up with an MVA out on the highway. Can you go over there and help him out?"

"Tell him I'm just a couple minutes away." Ian stood and grabbed his wallet from his back pocket, then tossed a five onto the table. "Duty calls," he said. "I'll see you later."

The squad car was parked in front of the diner, and as promised, it only took a minute for him to pull out into traffic and head over to Bay Street. Sally had been right. Cars were jammed in both directions, odd for a town that had only three stoplights. He left the patrol car at the back of the jam and hopped out, then walked up through the crowd of people and cars.

The majority of the people were gathered around Gallerie Luna, Marisol's shop. Ian groaned inwardly, surmising the cause of the congestion. As he approached, the crowd surged toward him, everyone talking at once, Mrs. Fibbler in the middle of the bunch. He held up his hands to quiet them. "I know what you're going to say. And I'll take care of it. Now everyone move along and get your day started."

"It's disgusting. Our children shouldn't have to look at that!"

"It's art!"

"Please. If that's art, then that parking meter over there is art."

"Ladies! Move along now. I told you, I'll take care of this."

When the crowd had cleared, he walked to the front door of the gallery and pressed the buzzer. At first, there was no answer, but then the door opened a crack and Marisol looked out. She smiled sleepily, squinting against the light. "Hi," she murmured. "What time is it?"

Ian glanced at his watch. "It's a little past eight."

She frowned. "In the morning?"

"Yeah," Ian said. "Can I come in?"

Marisol brushed her hair back, then rubbed her eyes. "Sure."

She stepped aside, then closed the door behind him. She was dressed in an oversize T-shirt that nearly reached her knees, hiding the tantalizing curves of her body. The shirt was covered with splotches of brightly colored paint. Her legs and feet were bare.

Ian found himself reacting the same way he had the first time he'd walked into her gallery. But he fought against the fantasies that tickled at his desire and focused on the business at hand. It wasn't easy. Marisol wore her beauty with a careless disregard for the effect it had on those around her. On him. Even in a T-shirt, with streaks of paint on her chin and hands, she was the most gorgeous creature he'd ever seen.

Dragging his gaze away from her face, Ian noticed the huge canvas propped up against the pillars in the center of the shop, and the ladder set in front of it. Wide swathes of orange and purple paint depicted a huge naked ass. "Nice," he murmured. "I'm glad to see you're trying something new."

"I was inspired," she said with a coy smile.

He thought back to the night before, to the intimacies they'd enjoyed, the crazy rush of passion that had swept them both away. Had he inspired her? "I'm afraid I'm going to have to ask you to change the window display. Today. It created a traffic jam on the street out front and that can't happen."

"You can't make me change it," Marisol said,

crossing her arms beneath her breasts and tipping her chin up defensively.

"Actually, now I can. It's a hazard to drivers and pedestrians. I can ticket you and for every day you keep it that way, the fine will increase."

Marisol gasped, then raked her hair out of her eyes. "You must be joking."

"No," Ian said. "I'm not. So, would you like me to write the ticket, or can I help you take those sculptures out of the window?"

She considered her options, glancing back and forth between him and the front window. Then, she sighed softly and held out her hand. "I'll take the ticket," she said.

"It's fifty dollars."

She glared at him, anger snapping in her dark brown eyes. "A small price to pay to maintain my artistic integrity."

Ian reached into his back pocket and withdrew his citation book, then wrote Marisol Arantes up on a violation of village ordinance 612.3. When he was finished, he handed her the ticket. "You can pay me right now, if you'd like. We take cash, checks or credit cards. Of course, you're still going to have to take the sculptures out of the window."

"I have no intention of paying you or removing the sculptures." She held the ticket under his nose then defiantly tore it into tiny pieces. They fluttered to the floor at his feet.

"All right," Ian said with a shrug. "Then I guess I've done my job."

"Too bad you can't say the same for last night," she muttered.

He stared at her, stung by the sarcastic challenge in her voice. "As I recall, that was a mutual decision."

"Was it?" she said.

He cursed softly, then, only to prove his point, he yanked her against his body, the instinct to kiss her again completely overwhelming him. His mouth came down on hers and he ran his hands beneath the T-shirt until they circled her waist. To his surprise, she was completely naked beneath. His brain told him to stop, but then she moaned and pressed her body against his, surrendering to the kiss.

Her skin was as soft and smooth as silk, her limbs perfectly formed. The moment he touched her, Ian wanted more, craving the feeling of something new and different. He would never be satisfied until he touched every inch of her skin, explored every gentle curve and every warm pulse point.

As it had been the night before, all sense of reality and propriety seemed to vanish. He forgot the citation, her refusal to follow his request, the reason for his visit in the first place. Every thought was focused on her body, on her reaction to his touch. He became consumed with the need to possess her, whether it be with a kiss or a caress or something much more intimate. Ian really didn't care. He wanted Marisol Arantes and whatever the consequences, he'd deal with them later.

Ian reached up and switched off his radio, then grabbed her waist and gently pulled her along to the worktable near the rear of the gallery. Without interrupting their kiss, he lifted her up on the table until she sat in front him. He drew back, then slowly pulled her T-shirt up and over her head.

The sight of her naked body took his breath away. He knew it would be perfect, but nothing had prepared him for the sheer beauty that she possessed. He reached for her breasts, cupping one in each hand and teasing at her nipples with his thumbs.

She watched him, her lips damp and slightly parted, her eyes half-closed. He ran his hands down her torso and over her hips, then reached behind her and shoved aside the papers and the tubes of paint scattered over the surface of the table. Gently, he pushed her back until she was lying in front of him.

He stepped between her legs, taking his time to explore her body with his hands and his lips. Marisol closed her eyes and surrendered to his touch, a smile curving the corners of her mouth. Ian wanted to strip off his own clothes and sink into her body. But he fought the temptation and instead, focused on pleasing Marisol.

He pressed a kiss to her belly, then moved lower, to the sweet spot between her legs. A tiny moan slipped from her throat as he ran his tongue along the soft folds of her labia. He parted her with his fingers then found her clitoris, gently caressing it with the tip of his tongue.

She arched against him, furrowing her fingers through his hair. He glanced up at her and saw the effect he was having, the flush of desire on her face, her bottom lip caught between her teeth. Ian had always been generous to his partners in bed, but this was something different.

He wanted her complete surrender, to know that at any moment he could possess her and she could do nothing to stop herself. Marisol's breath came in quick gasps, but Ian brought her along slowly, determined to prolong her pleasure.

And then, before he knew it, she was there, crying out as her body shuddered, grabbing the edge of the table with white-knuckled hands. Ian kissed the inside of each thigh, then took her hands and pulled her up. Gently, he smoothed the hair out of her eyes, tracing his fingers over the delicate arch of her eyebrow.

"Take me to bed," she murmured.

"Where do you sleep?" he asked.

She pointed up. "I have an apartment above the gallery."

Ian grabbed her T-shirt and tugged it over her head, then wrapped her legs around his waist and picked her up. He found the stairs behind the small kitchen. The apartment was sparsely furnished and filled with unpacked boxes. A rumpled bed stood in a corner below a bay window. He set Marisol on the mattress, then drew the covers up over her.

"Take your clothes off," she said.

"I can't," Ian replied. He bent over and dropped a kiss on her forehead. "I'm on duty."

Marisol groaned. "No, no. Call your boss and tell him you won't be in."

Ian chuckled. "I am the boss. I have to set the example. But I'll be back. Later."

Marisol rolled to her side and pushed up on her elbow, giving him a seductive smile. "We have some unfinished business."

He nodded, then bent over her and kissed her. "Pay that ticket, Miss Arantes, or the next time I see you, I'll have to slap the cuffs on you and drag you down to the station."

"I'll look forward to that," she teased.

Ian walked to the door, then looked back once before leaving. Marisol had already curled herself beneath the covers, her eyes closed. He shook his head. This was a helluva way to start his day.

A PERSISTENT RINGING woke her up from a delicious dream. Marisol rolled over in bed, brushing her hair out of her eyes. She stared at the clock for a long moment, then flopped back down into the pillow. Four o'clock. By the light shining through the windows, she could assume it was p.m., not a.m., and she hadn't missed the Templetons' party.

She hadn't slept so well in ages and there was no question about what had relaxed her. She smiled as she reached for the phone, hoping that it might be Ian. Perhaps she could convince him to return and finish what he'd begun. Marisol put the phone to her ear, expecting to hear his deep voice. "Hello?"

"This is National Express. We have a delivery for Marisol Arantes."

"That's me," she said, stifling a yawn. "From who?"

"It's a rather large crate, ma'am and we need your signature. We're out front."

Frowning, Marisol sat up. "I'll be right down." She wasn't expecting anything. All her paintings and sculptures had been shipped from New York last week and had arrived the day after she had. She grabbed a pair of paint-stained capris and tugged them on beneath the T-shirt.

When she opened the front door of the gallery, Marisol found a man waiting, dressed in the navy uniform of the delivery service. He handed her a clipboard and she signed her name, then he helped her slide the crate inside the door. As she dragged the crate across the floor, Marisol noticed that the sculptures she'd placed in the windows were now sitting in a tidy row along the wall.

She chuckled softly as she ripped open the packing slip. Mr. Law-and-Order had obviously decided to do the job himself before he left that morning. She set the crate aside, then grabbed the sculptures and placed them back into the window. If she couldn't win the battle between Ian and her body, then she wasn't about to give up on this fight.

When she returned to the crate, she noticed her father's name on the packing slip and smiled. Perhaps he'd changed his mind about showing his work in her gallery after all. Marisol ran her hand over the edge of the four-foot-square crate, then decided to open it later.

She was due at her very first Newport social event by 5:00 p.m., a cocktail reception at the estate of George and Cheryl Templeton. They'd been important clients of David's, and when they'd heard that Marisol was moving to the area, they'd insisted on setting up a small reception for her.

Marisol detested the business side of the art world, content to close herself up with her work and let it speak for itself. But unfortunately, most of the major collectors insisted on trotting out "their" artists and promoting careers that, in turn, would increase the value of the art they held.

George and Cheryl had been kind to offer their patronage and Sascha Duroy, Marisol's best friend, had promised to attend, so the evening wouldn't be all business and boredom. Sascha had a way of making even the most stuffy events amusing with her colorful stories and ribald sense of humor. Still, given the choice, Marisol would have preferred to stay home in the hopes that Ian might wander by and finish what he'd started earlier that morning.

She scolded herself silently. All her good intentions, all the promises she'd made to herself had suddenly evaporated in the presence of this man. But Marisol didn't need to fall in love with him to have a good time. And there was no doubt that Ian would be a very good time.

She glanced at the clock on the wall in the back of the gallery. The party began at four, but as the guest of honor, she wouldn't be expected to arrive before five. That meant she could stretch it to six.

The doorbell buzzed again and Marisol hurried back to the front of the gallery, wondering what the deliveryman had forgotten. Annoyance turned to anticipation as she realized Ian could be waiting, his workday over. But when she opened it, she found Sascha standing on the sidewalk, an impatient expression on her face.

"I knew I'd find you here," she said, bustling past Marisol. "I told Cheryl you'd be late, that you'd have some excuse about getting caught up in your work. So I decided to make sure you didn't embarrass us both by forgetting the party entirely. Get dressed. For once, I'm going to make sure you're on time."

Sascha Duroy was one of New York's most success-ful gallery owners and had many up-and-coming artists hanging in her gallery. She'd claimed to be thirty-seven on each of her last four birthdays, so Marisol assumed she was past forty by now. But with the aid of a very skilled plastic surgeon and good genes, Sascha barely looked thirty.

No matter where she was going—to the grocery store or to a reception at MoMA—Sascha always looked perfect, her nails done, her hair in place, her clothes tailored to within a millimeter of her well-toned figure. Marisol always looked as if she'd just rolled out of bed, combed her hair with her fingers and threw on the first thing that didn't have paint stains.

"I have to take a shower," she said. "And I don't have anything to wear."

Sascha raised her arm and a garment bag dangled from her finger. "I know," she said. "You love me. It's from Bergdorf and you'll look fabulous in it. And don't think of combing your hair. The bed-head look is perfect for you. It makes you seem just a tiny bit eccentric and they'll love you for it." Sascha handed her the garment bag. "Now, get ready. We're leaving in fifteen minutes. And try to look like you're going to enjoy yourself, darling. You need to work up some buzz about the gallery opening."

Marisol gave Sascha a reluctant smile, then ran upstairs to change. The silky slip dress was beautiful. Instead of the usual black, Sascha had chosen a lovely champagne color with delicate beading around the low neckline and on the tiny straps.

She stripped off her T-shirt and capris and slipped into the dress. It clung to every curve so underwear was impossible, but the skirt was just long enough to provide modest coverage. A pair of strappy ecru heels from her closet finished off the look. She searched through the boxes of clothes for her black pashmina shawl and threw it around her shoulders.

As she applied a bit of lipstick, Marisol paused and stared at herself in the mirror, her gaze falling to her mouth. She touched her lips, remembering the feel of Ian's mouth on hers, the taste of his tongue and the warm damp that he'd left behind. His skills hadn't stopped there and a warm sensation pulsed through her blood as she remembered the shattering orgasm she'd enjoyed.

Until a week ago, her life had been so sedate. But now, she had a new place to live, a new business to run and a new lover. A tiny shiver skittered down her spine. When would she see him again? Would he call her or were they supposed to meet by chance? Perhaps he'd walk by her gallery tonight with another excuse of insomnia.

She'd have to make sure Sascha didn't keep her out too late. If she saw him tonight, Marisol had every intention of finishing what they had begun that morning.

"Hurry," Sascha shouted up the stairs.

Marisol grabbed a small clutch and stuffed her lipstick and a comb inside, then gave herself one last look. Too bad Ian wasn't here, she mused. He'd definitely appreciate the dress, and the naked body beneath it. This was an outfit that could get a girl laid and she didn't want to waste it on the Town & Country set.

Sascha was waiting at the door when Marisol came back downstairs. She pointed at the crate. "Something new I haven't seen? Remember, I have first dibs on all your work."

"My father sent it," Marisol said as she searched for her keys. "I think he might be painting again."

"I've always loved his work," Sascha said. "If he needs a place to show, I'm sure I could find—"

Marisol giggled. "You and my father. You'd eat him alive. Besides, I don't think he can work at the pace that your considerable sales skills require of an artist."

Sascha's Volvo station wagon was parked out front, but Marisol insisted on taking her car, knowing she could leave whenever she wanted. She wrapped her shawl over her hair and tossed the ends around her shoulders, then started the car and pulled it out into traffic.

After a week, she'd learned enough about the area to find her way over the bridge and into Newport. But as she steered the car around a wide curve in the highway just outside of Bonnett Harbor, she heard a siren. Glancing into the rearview mirror, Marisol saw a squad car following her, lights flashing.

"Oh, shit," Sascha said. "What is this all about? You weren't speeding. Well, not that much."

"Don't worry," Marisol said. "This won't be a problem."

She pulled over to the side of the road and put the car in neutral, then waited. Marisol watched in the rearview mirror as Ian approached, his eyes hidden behind sunglasses, his face a mask of authority. She pushed the shawl off her hair and smiled up at him. "Hello, Officer," she said with a teasing tone. "I'm beginning to think you really are following me. I may have to get a restraining order."

Ian chuckled. "Yes, restraint. I think we could both use a little of that, don't you agree?"

"Was I breaking some law?"

"Are you aware that you were driving over the speed limit? I'm afraid I'm going to have to give you a ticket."

"Oh, dear," Marisol sighed, sending him a playful pout. "Another ticket. Well, we know how this went the last time you gave me a ticket. Can I count on it going the same way?"

A boyish smile quirked at the corners of his mouth and she knew exactly what he was thinking. He glanced up and down the road, then squatted down beside the door of her car. "I don't think that's appropriate for this location, Miss Arantes. We'd need a bit more privacy."

He pulled out his little ticket book, but this time she wasn't going to let him use it. There had to be some benefit to their "friendship." Marisol reached out and grabbed the front of his shirt and pulled him closer until his face was just inches from hers. "You moved my sculptures," she whispered.

"You ripped up my citation. I figured I was keeping you out of further trouble."

Marisol let go of his shirt, but he didn't step back. She smoothed her hand along his chest, toying with a button on the front of his uniform. "I put them back in the window where they belong."

Ian shrugged. "Then I'll be back to write you another ticket."

"Why waste your time writing out tickets? You're far more successful at other efforts," she said.

He took off his sunglasses and Marisol caught her breath as his gaze met hers. Those eyes, she mused. Every desire he felt was reflected in the blue depths. "Where are you going in that dress, Miss Arantes?" His gaze dropped to her chest. "Because that dress is definitely against the law."

"To a cocktail party. Would you like to come?" She paused. "To the party, I mean?"

"I'd love to come," he replied, making a careful examination of her lips. "To the party. But I'm not dressed for a party."

"Then go home and get dressed. I'll put your name on the guest list. It's in Newport at George and Cheryl Templeton's estate." She turned to Sascha. "Do you have the invitation?"

Sascha stared, confused and utterly speechless at the exchange between them. She fumbled in her purse and withdrew an envelope. Marisol handed the envelope to Ian. "Don't wear the uniform," she said. "But bring the handcuffs."

He grinned, then slipped his sunglasses on and walked back to the squad car. Marisol watched his retreat in the rearview mirror, admiring his easy stride and the fit of his uniform. A lot of men had modeled for her during her career so she'd become rather immune to the male form. But Ian's body intrigued her. She'd touched him, but she hadn't had a chance to just look…to breathe him in and let the beauty of his body burn into her brain. She'd had several very vivid fantasies about what might lie beneath the uniform and suddenly she felt desperate to know for sure.

"What was that all about?"

"Nothing," Marisol said. She waited for Ian to make a U-turn and head back into town, then she pulled back into traffic.

"Nothing? That was *not* nothing," Sascha sputtered. "That was something. And I want to know what it was."

"We've met before," Marisol explained.

"I would hope so. That's not the way one talks to strangers."

Marisol smiled slyly. "He's going to be my next lover," she said. "And it's going to be wonderful. And that's all I'm going to say."

"WOW, YOU LOOK SHARP." Sally stared at Ian as he walked into the station. "I don't think I've ever seen you in a tie. Don't tell me you have a date."

"You think it's too much?" Ian asked, turning to stare at his reflection in the window. "I'm going to a cocktail party. What the hell is that exactly? I've never been to a cocktail party. I'm not sure what they wear."

"It's summer, so it'll be pretty relaxed," Sally said. "You could probably get rid of the tie. And maybe even your socks. Loafers without socks are cool."

Ian glanced down at what he was wearing. He usually took his fashion cues from Declan, who spent enough time with rich people to know how to dress. Thankfully, Declan had left a closet full of clothes at Ian's house, just in case he didn't have time to drive back to his place in Providence before attending an event in Newport. The linen trousers were finely pressed and a nut-brown shirt and tan blazer had been clipped together in the dry cleaning bag so Ian took that as a cue that Dec had worn them at the same time.

"Did you get anywhere with the Penis Lady?" Sally asked.

"Don't call her that," Ian muttered as he unknotted the tie. "Her name is Marisol Arantes."

"Are you really going to let her show all those…bits and pieces in her front window?"

"She's an artist. It's freedom of speech. There's no law against it. In fact, I remember a few years back when a few of the old biddies in town wanted to put a dress on that naked statue in the lobby of the library and the village board said no."

"That was a woman," Sally said.

"We can't discriminate," Ian replied.

She frowned. "I suppose not. So what do you want me to do with all the calls?"

"Tell them I'm working on the problem. And if they have any more complaints they can call Ken Francis. He's the village president. Let him pass an ordinance."

Ian glanced over at the clock. It was nearly seven. He figured if he arrived late, he'd have a better chance of spending the rest of the night with Marisol. But he didn't want to arrive after the party was over. "This thing started at four," he said. "How long do you think it will last?"

"It all depends on the guests," Sally said. "If it's a good mix, it could go all night. From what I understand, the Templetons are known for their parties. My brother's wife's sister does their catering and she says Cheryl Templeton would throw a party every night if her husband would allow it."

Ian waved to Sally, then remembered the favor Marisol had requested. He hurried back to his office and grabbed his handcuffs, then shoved them into the waistband of his trousers, beneath his jacket. "You know where I'll be," he called as he walked out the front door of the station.

The ride over to Newport was slow going, a fender bender on the bridge bringing traffic to a halt. He glanced down at the clothes he wore and wondered what Declan would have to say about…his smile faded. Oh, hell, what if his brother was working the party tonight? Declan provided security for many of the big events in Newport. But this really wasn't an event, was it? A cocktail party was just a—

Ian cursed and banged his hand against the steering wheel. He'd made a pact with his brothers to stay away from women for the next three months. And he'd hadn't even lasted twenty-four hours. But they'd have to understand. When a woman as beautiful as Marisol Arantes comes along, a guy just can't walk away. She was a once-in-a-lifetime, the kind of woman he'd still be talking about years from now.

The idea behind the pact had been valid. Taking a break from the opposite sex could provide some valuable perspective. But he'd been in the midst of a five-month drought when they'd made the deal and he hadn't experienced any miraculous revelations in that time. He'd enjoy Marisol for as long as she'd have him, guilt free, and if the time came, he'd pay his brothers for the pleasure.

The sun was beginning to set when he pulled onto Ruggles Avenue and drove toward the water. The address was easy enough to find and Ian took some small comfort that the party wasn't in one of Newport's largest "cottages." But he still couldn't help but feel a bit out of place as he steered the Mustang up the circular drive.

A valet ran out to take the keys and Ian pasted a smile on his face as he walked to the door. If Dec was here, he'd have to come up with a plausible excuse for his invitation. But to his relief, the guy at the door discreetly checked the invitation and asked Ian's name, then encouraged him to have a pleasant evening.

Music drifted in from the terrace and Ian wandered through the elegant house, snagging a glass of champagne from a passing waiter. Paintings hung in every available spot and Ian stopped and stared at a colorful depiction of two horses, appreciating the power of the painter's vision. He searched the room, looking for something he'd recognize as Marisol's, but the Templetons seemed to prefer animals to naked men.

Wide French doors lined the back side of the house, providing a beautiful view of the ocean just past the Cliff Walk. Ian stood in the doorway, sipping his champagne and observing the small clusters of guests enjoying their drinks and eating hors d'oeuvres in the warm summer night.

The only time he ever came in contact with these people was when they wandered across the bay to shop in Bonnett Harbor. Bonnett Harbor couldn't boast a single 30,000-square-foot summer cottage or even a few billionaire citizens. It offered just enough to tempt the tourists across the bridge for an afternoon of shopping or a nice dinner at one of the town's many restaurants.

"Nice view."

The voice sent a shiver through his body and Ian slowly turned to find Marisol watching him from a nearby doorway. His gaze drifted from her face to her feet and back again.

"I like my view better," he said, chuckling softly. "That dress is definitely going to get you in trouble." The way it clung to her body, he was certain she wore nothing beneath it. He could see the curves of her breasts, her nipples as they pressed against the fabric and the sweet spot between her legs as she leaned against the door.

She crooked her finger at him and Ian walked across the room. Grabbing his hand, Marisol pulled him through the doorway and into a wide hall. They walked past the main stairway and Marisol opened another door and pulled him inside a tiny powder room built beneath the stairs. As soon as she locked the door, she turned to him and began to unbutton his shirt.

Ian leaned back against the edge of the sink and watched her, his heart slamming in his chest, unwilling, or perhaps unable, to stop her. Her hair brushed against his chin and he smiled as the scent of her perfume wafted up to his nose. "What are you doing?" he asked.

"Undressing you," she said.

"Why?"

"I have to." She shoved his jacket and shirt off his shoulders at the same time. Ian reached behind himself to unbutton the cuffs, then let the clothes slide to the floor. She immediately began on his trousers, unbuckling his belt and working the zipper open.

When she slid them down, the handcuffs clattered to the floor unnoticed. Ian kicked off his shoes and stood in his bare feet, left in just his boxers.

Marisol stepped back, to the far wall of the bathroom, her hands clenched at her sides. "Now the rest," she said.

Ian shook his head. "What are we doing here?"

"I have to see you," she said. "Naked. I just have to. Humor me."

Ian wasn't sure what kind of game they were playing now, but she seemed dead serious. Her brow was furrowed and her breath came in quick little gasps. He reached for the waistband of his boxers, then slowly slid them down to his ankles.

Ian straightened, bracing his hands behind him on the edge of the sink. He'd been so surprised by her behavior that he hadn't had time to react. But now, as her gaze drifted over his body, he felt a rush of heat course through his veins. Ian glanced down and watched as he grew harder with each passing second.

"You're beautiful," she murmured, a tiny smile curving her lips. "I knew you would be." Slowly, she crossed the space between them, then reached out and ran her hand over his chest. Her fingers slowly outlined each muscle, as if she were making a scientific study rather than beginning a seduction.

Her fingers dipped lower, to explore his belly, and then even lower still. The moment she brushed against his erection, Ian sucked in a sharp breath. Her hand stilled for a heartbeat, her gaze fixed on his crotch. Ian wasn't sure what she had in mind, but the curiosity was just about killing him.

Marisol slowly sank to her knees in front of him, her gaze still fixed in one spot, her hands exploring every detail. He closed his eyes and tipped his head back, hoping that she didn't intend to stop. If this was one of the activities usually practiced at cocktail parties, then he'd have to attend many more.

He watched as her lips came closer. The wait was excruciating but it was sweet torture, the kind that made the anticipation as much fun as what was about to come. He reached out and ran his fingers through her hair.

What act of fate had put this woman in his life? He felt as if he'd been caught up in some fantasy. Things like this—women like Marisol—just didn't happen to him.

Ian closed his eyes and drew a deep breath as her hands circled his hips to smooth over his buttocks. And then, she kissed him, her lips damp against the base of his penis. He groaned softly as she worked her way up the length of his shaft. If this was a dream, if he was somehow asleep, he'd feel like a fool later. But awake or asleep, he planned to enjoy it.

Her tongue danced over the tip of his erection, sending currents of pleasure racing through his body. When she took him inside her mouth, the shock of her caress made his knees weak. Ian had enjoyed this particular act many times in the past, but he'd never felt such an intense connection to his reactions. Or to the woman causing them.

Every movement brought him closer to the edge, but he fought it, wanting these strange and wonderful sensations to last. He looked down, but the sight of her, kneeling in front of him, her lips surrounding him, only brought him closer to completion, his orgasm just a heartbeat away.

A knock sounded on the door, but Marisol didn't seem to notice. "Busy," he called, his voice cracking slightly. And then, from out of nowhere, the orgasm hit him, sending a deep shudder through his body. He stifled a cry and tried to stop the spasms, but then realized that he didn't want to.

She took him in, continuing to surround him with her

tongue and her lips, sapping him of every last bit of his desire. When it was finally finished, Ian looked down at her and found her smiling, satisfied that she'd pleasured him well. She ran her tongue over him one last time, then slowly stood.

"You're making me crazy," he murmured, breathless and spent.

She reached for the glass of champagne he'd set on the sink and took a long sip, then placed a kiss on the center of his chest. "Get dressed," she said. "I'll meet you outside."

With that, Marisol slipped out of the bathroom. Ian quickly reached over and locked the door again, then drew a long, deep breath. Hell, if he had to pay his brothers ten thousand to break their celibacy pact he would. He intended to have as much of Marisol Arantes as he wanted and he wasn't about to put a price on that kind of pleasure.

3

"He certainly is handsome."

Marisol nodded as she watched Ian converse with a small group of men. She wasn't sure what they were discussing, but they seemed to be engaged in a very animated debate. In truth, she was surprised he fit in so easily. The society crowd could be closed-minded and judgmental at times. But Ian didn't seem impressed by the wealth or position of the people around him and they didn't question who he was or why he'd been invited to the party.

"I guess, when I moved to Bonnett Harbor, I really didn't expect to find anyone that interesting," she murmured.

"And is he interesting?" Sascha asked, raising an eyebrow inquisitively.

Marisol nodded. "He's different. He doesn't have an agenda, he's just who he is," she added.

"Unlike David?"

She winced at the mention of his name. "Maybe," Marisol replied. "It really doesn't matter, though, because I'm just using him for sex." The minute the words were out of her mouth, she regretted saying them.

Perhaps it was the truth, but she respected Ian enough not to take their attraction lightly. It wasn't just the physical connection they shared that fascinated her. There was something more to this man, something hidden beneath the surface that she found undeniably attractive. She hadn't known him long enough to define what it was.

Sascha took a sip of her champagne as she scanned the guests on the terrace. "Speaking of lying, cheating scumbags, I spoke with David a few days ago. He and the Brazilian have parted ways. He actually admitted that conversation with her was such a chore he couldn't stand her any longer. And, he asked how you were doing. I think he might give you a call. In fact, I expected him to turn up here tonight."

There had been a time, before she'd met Ian, when Sascha's revelation would have thrilled her. But now, Marisol felt nothing but mild annoyance. How could she possibly care what David said or thought when she had Ian to occupy her fantasies? "When you see him again, tell him I'm not interested."

Sascha frowned. "You said it yourself, Mari. This Quinn is a temporary thing, so why close the door on David? You two were so good together."

"Looking back on it, I don't think we were," Marisol said. In truth, she and Ian were much better together and they barely knew each other.

"You're just saying that because you're all caught up in this new man. Everything is very exciting. But this passion will fade, you know it will."

Marisol nodded, but she couldn't completely agree with Sascha's statement. There was something about the way Ian touched her, the way he made her feel, that seemed to hold so much promise. Their attraction was a mystery and no matter how she looked at it, it didn't make much sense. He wasn't the type of man she usually found herself falling for.

But then, maybe that *was* the answer. She wasn't falling for him. She was simply infatuated, as Sascha had said, swept away by the growing intimacy between them and by the fantasies yet to be explored.

"Have I stayed here long enough?" Marisol asked.

"Have you talked to everyone, introduced yourself and told them about the opening?"

She nodded, then reached into her purse and found her car keys, handing them to Sascha. "Can you make it back on your own?"

"And how are you getting home?"

Marisol nodded to Ian. "Park the car in front of the gallery and put the keys behind the potted tree to the left of the door."

Sascha leaned closer and gave Marisol a peck on both cheeks. "Be careful. You don't know much about this man. Don't trust him so easily, all right? After that mess with David, you didn't work for three months. I can't afford you falling into a funk—and neither can you."

Marisol walked away from Sascha, her attention now fixed firmly on Ian. He looked so different in the jacket and pressed shirt. Though it wasn't as sexy as the uniform, it made him look less imposing, more approachable. He'd combed his hair, but the evening breeze had messed it up, the dark waves falling over his forehead. As she joined him, she fought the urge to reach up and brush the hair out of his eyes.

"Has everyone here been introduced to Marisol?" he asked, resting his hand on the small of her back. He made a few introductions and she listened distractedly, her attention focused on his hand. The simple yet possessive gesture sent a rush of warmth through her body and she held her breath as he let his palm drift slightly lower.

As they listened to the conversation, she imagined his thoughts were on seduction and not on the subject of the discussion, the current state of the stock market. Ian's hand drifted up and down her back as he smoothed his palm against the silk dress, the sensations driving her mad with the need to touch him in return.

"Will you excuse us?" she suddenly said, taking Ian's arm. They hurried back toward the house, Marisol pulling him along behind her.

"Are we going to the bathroom again?" Ian asked, offering slight resistance.

"We're getting out of here," she replied. "I'm tired, my feet hurt, and I can't talk about myself any longer. These people bore me to death." She turned to him. "And I have this overwhelming need to get naked with you. You don't bore me."

It was so easy with Ian, she mused. She didn't hesitate to tell him exactly what she wanted. Maybe it was because he wanted the same thing. But it wasn't just sex and the act of pleasuring each other that she enjoyed. It was the intimacy, the feeling that at the very moment he surrendered, she knew him better than any woman on the planet.

When they reached the privacy of the house, Marisol wrapped her arms around his neck and kissed him, her tongue offering a taste of temptation, her body molding to his. "It was nice of you to come," she said as his hand skimmed along her spine to cup her backside. "But I think we should leave now."

"Are you sure?" Ian asked. He kissed her again and again, short, sweet kisses all around her mouth, his breath coming in little gasps, his eyes shadowed with desire. They stumbled back into a dark corner, laughing softly as Marisol's hand brushed the front of his linen trousers.

"Positive."

"We'd better get out of here before we get caught," he murmured as spun her around. "I do have a reputation to maintain."

"And I don't?" Marisol teased.

"You make sculptures of naked men. And you don't wear underwear. I think people expect you to be a little wild."

"There's only one thing to do then," she said, turning away from him. "I must find a way to ruin your reputation."

"There you are!" Ian and Marisol jumped apart as Cheryl Templeton hurried into the room, flushed from too much champagne. She grabbed them both. "You're not leaving? It's early."

Ian cleared his throat, then moved Marisol in front him,

obviously embarrassed by the erection that pressed against his trousers. "Marisol has a lot of work to do before her opening," he explained. "And I have to get back."

"Oh, pooh," Cheryl said. "Well, before you leave, I have to show you our new acquisition. Come, it's in the library."

She hurried ahead of them and Ian took Marisol's hand, weaving his fingers through hers. They walked past the bathroom beneath the stairs and Ian made to pull her inside, but Marisol sent him a warning glare and dragged him back into the hallway.

"George hates it, but I love it," Cheryl said, staring at the abstract oil. "Emory Colter's work has grown so much in popularity over the past ten years that we paid far more for it than we intended. But I don't care."

She stood in front of Marisol and Ian and chattered on and on about the painting, about their art collection, about the artists she'd entertained. He bent close and dropped a kiss on Marisol's bare shoulder, his lips warm and damp. She pulled away, but Ian moved behind her and wrapped his hands around her waist, smoothing his palms along her hips, then around to her belly and lower.

The silk provided no protection from his touch, the heat of his hands burning into skin. Marisol closed her eyes and leaned back against him as his hands moved up to cup her breasts. She didn't care that there was another person in the room, yet she was aware that any moment Mrs. Templeton would turn around and see what was happening.

Why was she so defenseless against his touch? When he put his hands on her body, she lost the ability to think for herself. He took control and she was happy to surrender. Through half-hooded eyes, she watched their hostess, waiting for her to move and recognize what was going on behind her.

Ian's thumbs brushed across her nipples, bringing them to hard peaks. Marisol reached back and ran her hands along his hips, rubbing against his erection, the silk transmitting the warmth and feel of him.

Suddenly, she regretted her decision not to duck into the bathroom. Any show of resistance was silly at this point. The attraction between them had become wildly overwhelming and she loved the way it made her feel— alive with excitement, as if every breath she took was filled with a hunger that begged to be sated.

When he touched her, or simply looked at her, she could think of nothing but tearing his clothes off and enjoying the pleasure of his body. And there were many pleasures to enjoy—his wide shoulders and narrow waist, his flat belly with the tiny trail of dark hair that led to temptations below. He had a small birthmark above his right hip and a scar on his left shoulder, just a few details she remembered from their time in the bathroom. But Marisol wanted more that just a map of his body. She wanted the key to his passion.

What made his heart pound, what made his desire for her burn? Did he like to be kissed in a certain way, was there something in her touch that made him hard and ready? And what would he feel when he finally moved inside her, when his orgasm overwhelmed him?

There were so many things she needed to know and

she was impatient to learn it all, first in bed and then by sculpting him. Already, she could imagine Ian standing before her, quiet, still, relaxed and completely naked. But this time, she could touch him as she worked, run her hands along his flanks, explore the perfect curve of his backside and examine the beautiful line from his hip to his ankle.

"Well, I'm sure I'm boring you both to death." Mrs. Templeton slowly turned and Ian's hands immediately returned to his sides. Marisol felt a warm flush creep up her cheeks and was glad for the low lighting in the room.

"It's a lovely piece," Marisol said.

"And I can't wait to get a look at your new work," Cheryl countered. "Your friend here has been singing your praises all night."

"Yes, well, I'm not getting much done lately," Marisol explained, surprised that Ian had been talking about her. "And I really should work tonight." She held out her hand. "Thank you for everything and would you say my goodbyes?"

Cheryl nodded, and when Ian reached around Marisol, she took his hand as well, then led them both out to the foyer before bidding them good night.

Ian and Marisol stood at the driveway while the valet retrieved Ian's car, their fingers tangled together, Marisol's thoughts focused on the rest of the evening. She was past playing coy games. When they got back to the gallery, she'd take him inside, tear his clothes off and force him to make love to her. She smiled to herself. She couldn't imagine that he'd refuse.

When the valet pulled up in front of them, Ian walked around to the passenger side of the convertible and helped her in. They drove out the driveway and through Newport in silence, the warm night air soft on her skin. Marisol glanced his way every so often, trying to discern his thoughts. A tiny smile was the only hint he gave and she nervously toyed with her evening bag, snapping the clasp open and shut.

If everything followed as it had begun, he would stay with her tonight—and it would be wonderful, their naked bodies lying together, hands and mouths exploring until they both reached the point of no return and then the wild rush of pleasure as he moved inside of her.

Marisol took a deep breath and closed her eyes. She'd drunk too much champagne, but her head felt perfectly clear, every sense piqued, every nerve on edge.

"Are you tired?" he asked.

Marisol turned to find him looking at her. "No. Not at all."

"So, you need to work tonight?"

"No," she murmured. "I was just saying that because I wanted to leave."

His smile widened and he fixed his gaze on the road ahead. Marisol didn't even notice when they reached Bonnett Harbor or when he turned down Bay Street to the gallery. When the car stopped, she waited for Ian to come around and open her door.

He grabbed her hand and pulled her out of the car, then held out his hand. "Keys," he said. But he didn't wait for them. Instead, he pulled her into the shadows of the doorway and kissed her. "Keys," he repeated.

Marisol drew back to search through her purse, then remembered. "No keys," she said. "I gave them to Sascha." She moaned. "And she likes to be the last one at the party. We'll have to go back and get them."

"No time," Ian said, his voice low and seductive. "Come with me."

"Where are we going? We can't go to your place. You have your reputation to protect."

"I know a place."

They got back in the car and Ian drove toward the water. When they reached the bottom of Harbor Street, he turned left and drove along the docks, then turned again in front of a sign that advertised Quinn's Boatworks. "My father's business," he said, nodding at the sign. When he reached a chain-link gate, he hopped out of the car and unlocked it, then drove the car through.

"Where are we?" she asked.

"Wait," he murmured as he locked the gate behind them.

They pulled over a small rise and Ian turned off the lights and the ignition, then coasted to a stop. She stared out across the waters of Narragansett Bay. In the distance, the lights of Newport twinkled. Just above the horizon, the moon shone brightly.

"We're alone," Ian murmured as he jumped out of the car. "This is the boat landing for my dad's boatyard.

The only way down here is through that gate. It's completely private."

He helped her out. "It's beautiful," Marisol said.

They walked around to the front of the car and Ian lifted her up to sit on the hood. He stepped between her legs and took her face in his hands. "You're beautiful." He kissed her gently. "And you're making me crazy, Marisol," he continued, his breath hot on her neck. "All I do is think about you…about this. All day long, I can feel you on my hands and taste you in my mouth."

"I'm sorry," Marisol said, arching back, her hands braced behind her.

"Don't be." He yanked her closer, then ran his hand from her collarbone to her belly and back again. "I can't stop touching you. I don't want to."

She closed her eyes. "Maybe we shouldn't do this. Maybe it's too soon." But her words weren't a warning, simply a test to see just how far he was willing to go for pleasure. She reached for his belt and began to work at the buckle.

"I'm the one who shouldn't do this," he said, brushing the straps of her dress aside. "I made a deal with my brothers."

She yanked the belt out of his pants and tossed it over her shoulder into the car. "You made a deal?"

"No sex, no women for three months. My idiot brother thought it would be a good idea." He pressed her back on the hood and kissed her neck, trailing kisses across her shoulder. "He thought it might help us understand women."

"And has it worked?"

"No." Ian reached down for the hem of her dress and drew it up, then groaned softly. "Do you ever wear underwear?"

"Only when absolutely necessary," she said. She furrowed her fingers through his hair and pulled him into another kiss, her head spinning. Every nerve in her body was on fire and his touch was the only thing that could soothe the burn.

He found the spot between her legs and she groaned, watching him in the moonlight. "You don't need to stop having sex to understand women," she said. "I think you understand woman just fine."

"Do I?" He slipped his finger inside of her, once and then twice, and then began a tantalizing rhythm, teasing at her clitoris with each stroke.

"You know what I want, don't you?" she said in a ragged voice.

"I do," he replied. "I'm just not sure when."

"Now would be good," she said. She slid off the hood of the car and stood in front of him, slowly unbuttoning his shirt. Marisol smoothed her hands over his chest, a light dusting of hair slipping between her fingers. "I came prepared," she said. She walked around the car and fetched her purse, then pulled out a condom.

Chuckling, Ian reached for his wallet and retrieved a plastic packet. "So did I."

She snapped her purse shut and tossed it back into the car, then grabbed the condom from him. Holding it between her teeth, she finished undoing his trousers, desperate to feel him inside of her. Marisol didn't want to bother with foreplay, not now. She hooked her fingers in the waistband of his boxers and pulled them down.

When he was exposed to the night air, she tore the condom open and then deftly sheathed him, his penis hot and hard. He closed his eyes and held his breath, as if he were already close to the edge. Then, grabbing the lapels of his jacket, Marisol pushed him down on the hood of the car and straddled him.

For a long moment, she waited, knowing that if she wanted to stop now, she could. But that was as far as her control went, just a casual thought and nothing more. His erection brushed against her damp entrance and Marisol's need overwhelmed her. Slowly, she lowered herself, burying him inch by delicious inch, deep inside of her, in one long, sensuous movement.

There was just enough light to watch his face, to see the odd mixture of pain and pleasure etched across it. This was what she had wanted from the moment she'd set eyes on Ian Quinn, but now that she had it—had him—Marisol was afraid to move, afraid that the reality wouldn't live up to her fantasies.

Ian grabbed her hips and silently begged her to keep still. But she rocked forward to kiss him and he slipped out of her. Marisol sighed as she sank down on top of him again, acutely aware of every sound, his breathing, the low moans he made as she moved, the crickets chirping and the waves against the concrete apron of the boat landing.

"Wait," he murmured, holding her back again. "Slower."

She sat up, then tipped her face into the moonlight. He filled her so completely, so perfectly that with every stroke, he brought her closer to the edge. She reached down and grabbed the hem of her dress and pulled it up over her head, the warm breeze caressing her naked skin.

Ian let out a long slow breath and stared at her, his expression cast in dark shadows and soft light. He reached between them and touched her and Marisol moved again, this time more carefully, so they could both enjoy the pleasure they were giving each other.

As she drove him deep inside her, Marisol let go of conscious thought and focused on the desire building. Instinct took over and she moved toward it with a single-minded urgency, pulling Ian along with her. And then, in a split second, she was there on the edge. She opened her eyes and looked down at him, only to find his gaze fixed on her face.

Like a wave washing over her, knocking her off her feet, the pleasure was nearly unbearable. A spasm rocked her body and she arched against him and Ian joined her, holding her still as he came. It had taken so little time, yet Marisol had never experienced such a powerful reaction with a man.

Their orgasms seemed to last forever, Ian shuddering beneath her until he was completely spent. He threw his arms over his head and groaned softly as she continued to move. Then Marisol collapsed on his chest, her fingers and toes tingling and her mind hazy.

Ian raked his fingers through her hair, pulling it away

from her face so he could kiss her forehead. "Are you all right?" he asked, his heart thudding wildly beneath her ear.

"Mmm," Marisol murmured. "I'm perfect."

He stared up at the sky, slowly stroking her back. "You are," he whispered. "Perfect for me."

Marisol pushed up on her elbow and dropped a gentle kiss on his lips. "If I ask you something, will you promise to say yes?"

"Yes," Ian said. "Now tell me what I've agreed to."

"I want you to pose for me. I want to sculpt you. Will you do that?"

"Will I have to take my clothes off?"

"Of course," Marisol said.

"All right. But only if you agree to take your clothes off, too."

"I'm not sure we'd get a lot done if we were both naked."

Ian chuckled and ran his finger along her bottom lip. "I wouldn't be too sure about that. We seem to do our best work with our clothes off."

MARISOL STOOD in front of the easel, staring at the canvas, a stream of sunlight spilling into the gallery from the windows along the back wall. She'd been working on the painting since Ian had left her in the early-morning hours before dawn. She'd expected to be exhausted by the passion they'd enjoyed with each other, but the moment he drove off, Marisol felt exhilarated, as if all her energy had been recharged.

Funny what a few really good orgasms could do for a

girl, she mused, unable to keep from smiling. And they had been good, deep, powerful and mindless, shaking her to her very core. Even now, thinking of what they'd shared, Marisol's blood warmed and her pulse quickened. She could live like this forever, without sleeping, needing only her work and sex with Ian Quinn to sustain her.

She thought back to the kiss he'd given her at the door, knowing it would have to last her at least another twelve hours. Now every minute away from him seemed empty and unexciting.

Their affair had begun as a playful little game between two consenting adults, simple and easy sex, nothing serious. But after last night, Marisol had been forced to reevaluate. She'd never been with a man who'd made her feel the way Ian did. And it wasn't just the orgasms. It was the way he looked at her and touched her, as if she were the perfect woman for him, the only woman who could bring him to complete satisfaction.

So many of the men in her life had tried to change her, to make her into someone who played by the rules. Even David hadn't been satisfied, constantly harping on her crazy work schedule and chaotic approach to her art and her distaste for self-promotion. In all truth, he'd never wanted to be with a working artist, he'd wanted an interesting woman on his arm, someone who could talk the talk that he enjoyed so much.

It was nice not to have to discuss her work with Ian. He saw it, he admired it, and that was all. She dabbed a bit more blue on her brush and added a touch to the eyes. It wasn't a realistic representation of a man, but an abstract figure that mirrored her emotional reaction to their passion.

She'd painted him as she'd seen him last night, standing before her in the moonlight, naked and unfazed, his gaze downcast, his head tilted slightly. Marisol was amazed at how easy it had been to meld color with form, the memory of him burned into her brain like a sharply focused photograph.

In real life, he looked like a modern-day Greek god, all muscle and sinew, hard angles and strong curves. On the canvas, he was brilliant color and vibrant slashes of paint, seductive strength and devastating power.

As she stared at the painting, she couldn't help but think of the man and wonder what he was doing at that moment. Was he thinking about her? Did her taste still linger in his mouth? Could he still feel the imprint of her hands on his body? Had thoughts of their night together plagued his day as they had hers?

The buzzer sounded at the gallery's front door and Marisol turned and smiled, then wiped her paint-stained fingers on her dress. "Just in time," she murmured.

She ran to the door and threw it open, anxious to kiss him, to slowly undress him and make love for the next five or six hours. But she didn't find Ian waiting. Instead, Sascha stood in the doorway, staring at her over the top of her Chanel sunglasses. "I brought you lunch, though it's nearly dinner time." She swept past Marisol then turned and frowned. "What have you done to your new dress?"

Marisol glanced down, not realizing that she'd forgotten to change. Globs of paint clung to the pale silk, red and orange and black, the colors of desire. "Oh, no. I'm sorry. I wasn't thinking. As soon as I got home I started to work and I—" She rubbed her hands over the spots, then tried to chip them off with her fingernails. But the silk was ruined. "I'll pay you for the dress, I promise."

Sascha waved her hand. "Let me see what you've been doing." She followed Marisol over to the painting, then studied it. "It's quite good." She drew a deep breath, then sighed. "It's very good. It's… stirring."

"It is, isn't it," Marisol said, excitement filling her voice. "I think it's the best work I've done in a long time. I really captured the essence of masculine power. It just seems to vibrate from him, don't you think?"

"Are we talking about the painting or Ian Quinn? Or are they one and the same?"

"Don't say it like that," she said, pouting. "Like he's some bad habit I ought to break. I have everything under control. Besides, I think this might be good for me. I feel energized. I can hardly wait to get to work." Marisol walked over to the crate her father had sent her and ran her hand along the top edge. "Maybe he's my muse."

"Please," Sascha scoffed. "You've never believed in that."

"I've never had a muse before," Marisol countered. "All I know is that after I'm with him, my work is more…focused. All my insecurities are gone and I can just create without even thinking. He makes me believe I'm a good painter and a good sculptor. And as long as that continues, I'm happy."

Sascha wandered over to stand next to her, bending down to peer through the slats of the crate. "What do you suppose is inside?"

Marisol shrugged. "I'm almost afraid to look. If it's bad, I'll have to lie to my father and tell him it's good. And if it's good, I'll tell him it's good and he'll refuse to believe me."

Sascha walked over to the worktable and grabbed the small crowbar that hung from the edge. "Let's put an end to your misery right now." She pried off the front of the crate, then removed the four-by-four-foot canvas, carefully brushing aside the packing material. As the layers of paper fell away, Marisol could see the basic colors and outlines of the painting and a sick feeling began to grow in her stomach.

"Oh, shit," Sascha murmured, when the last bit of wrapping was brushed aside. "I know this painting."

Marisol slowly dropped to the floor, running her hand over the surface of the canvas. "Oh, Papi, what have you done now?"

The signature on the painting was unmistakable and could lead her to only one conclusion. The Emory Colter hanging in the Templetons' library was a clever forgery and her father, until recently, had been in possession of the original.

"It's the same, isn't it?" Marisol murmured, desperate to have Sascha contradict her.

"It looks like your father might be up to his old tricks again," Sascha said.

"It's not just the second in a series?"

Sascha shook her head. "No, this is the same painting that Cheryl Templeton was showing off last night. Everyone at the party saw it. I can't believe that was a forgery. My God, if your father painted the fake, it's an amazing job. Emory Colter is not an easy artist to forge. His brush strokes and the application of paint to the canvas are so unique."

"This could be the forgery," Marisol said. "We don't know for sure."

"Why would your father send you a forged painting?" She shook her head. "You picked a bad time to start hanging around with a cop," Sascha commented. "And there's more bad news."

Marisol covered her eyes with her hands. "I don't want to hear it."

"David is the one who sold the Colter to the Templetons."

"You think he and my father are working together?"

"He's the one who authenticated it, Mari. Either he's slipping at his job, or he and your father are in this together. I'd put my money on the latter."

Marisol pushed to her feet and began to pace the floor in front of the painting. "I'm not going to jump to conclusions. I don't know that the painting in the Templetons' library is a fake. This could be the copy. And who knows why he painted it?" She groaned, then covered her face with her hands. "What am I going to do? Papi must have sent it here to hide it. Fake or real, if he gets caught with this, he'll be sent back to jail in a heartbeat."

"What are *you* going to do? This is not your problem, Marisol, it's your father's."

She grabbed Sascha's arm and squeezed it tight. "You have to promise not to tell anyone about this. Not until I figure out how to fix it."

"What can you do? You have to get rid of the painting. You can't keep it here."

"It's an Emory Colter, maybe. I can't sell it, I won't give it away, and I certainly will not destroy it. There's no way to get rid of it. Unless…"

"Unless?"

"If it is the real thing, I could exchange it for the fake," Marisol said. "I could find a way to get into the Templetons' estate and switch paintings. Then I could destroy the forgery and they'd be left with the real one. It wouldn't be difficult. It would take me just a few minutes to switch them."

"What if they have security?" Sascha said. "You don't think that painting is wired to some alarm? They have at least a couple million in artwork in that house and it's certainly not hanging there ready to be plucked off the wall."

"I could just leave it at the front door. And they'd figure it out."

"Your father's fingerprints could be all over that canvas. You need to exchange the two if there's any chance of keeping him out of this. But until you know which is which, you'd better stay away from Ian Quinn."

At that very moment, the buzzer rang and they both turned to look at the front door, then looked at each other. "Do you think that's him?" Marisol asked.

"Don't answer it. Pretend you're not here."

"He knows I'm here. My car is parked out front. I'll just talk to him for a minute and get him to go away. He saw the Colter at the Templetons' and he'll probably recognize it if he saw it again. You wrap it up and hide it in the storeroom and I'll…get rid of him."

Sascha picked up one of Marisol's T-shirts and tossed it at her. "Put this on. You'll never get rid of him wearing that dress."

Marisol did as ordered, then hurried to the front door. She peered through the blinds to see that Ian was indeed standing in front of the store, a large grocery bag held in his arms. Her heart skipped a few beats and she took a deep breath to try to still her hammering pulse.

It wasn't fair. She shouldn't have to make this choice, between her father's future and her affair with Ian. But there was no decision to consider. Her father was family. Ian was her lover, a man she barely knew.

"You can do this," Marisol murmured to herself.

IAN STOOD ON THE SIDEWALK and waited for Marisol to open the door. At first he'd wondered if she was home, but then he saw her peek through the blinds. He'd been waiting all day to get back to her, and though he was exhausted from lack of sleep, he had no intention of spending his evening home alone.

The door slowly opened and he smiled as she poked her head out. "Hi," she said.

"Hi," he replied. He looked at her for a long moment,

his gaze taking in all the tiny details of her face. When they'd first met, he'd considered her beautiful, but the more he got to know Marisol, the more he believed that he'd never meet another woman quite like her. "I brought dinner."

"Thank you," she said. "I—I'd ask you in, but I'm in the middle of something."

"Work?"

"Yes. Work."

She seemed nervous, uneasy in his presence. "Are you all right?" he asked. "You're not—"

"What? No, I'm fine. Everything is fine," she said. "I'm just tired. And busy. With work."

"Well, maybe you should take a break," Ian suggested. "Why don't you come out with me? We'll walk down to the waterfront and have a picnic. I have sandwiches and root beer."

"I'm really not dressed. And I look terrible."

"You look lovely," Ian said.

"I—I suppose you could come in for just a while. But then I really have to get back to work." She opened the door to let him pass. The front of the gallery was dimly lit, but light streamed in through the transoms above the door and the display windows, sending shafts of sunlight across the wood floor.

He set the bag down, then turned to Marisol, frowning. "You seem—"

"What? I'm fine," she said.

"Preoccupied," he finished. "If there's something wrong, we should probably talk about it. You can be straight with me Marisol. We're certainly not in a position where we have to hide anything from each other."

She laughed softly, but the sound was forced. "There are always things to hide."

"Do you regret what happened last night?"

Marisol shook her head. "No. Not at all."

A rush of relief came over him and Ian crossed the distance between them and took her in his arms. "Good." He bent and kissed her and she offered no resistance. Instead, she seemed to melt against him. Her lips parted and he drank deeply of her taste, like a man dying of thirst in the desert. When he finally drew back, Ian noticed that her face was flushed and eyes clouded with desire.

"You look tired," he said.

"I haven't slept since you dropped me off."

Ian frowned. "You're going to run yourself down and then you're going to get sick." He took her hand, then grabbed the bag. "Come on. Let's get you some dinner and then I'm going to put you to bed."

"I can take care of myself," Marisol said.

"I'm sure you can. But you aren't."

She grabbed his arm and pulled him back, then practically jumped into his arms and kissed him. Ian couldn't explain her odd behavior except that she did look exhausted. He dropped the bag on the floor and slipped his hands around her waist, picking her up off her feet until her body slid along his.

He felt himself grow hard with just the brief contact and he pressed her back against the wall and skimmed his hands over her body, his mind already on the pleasures of sex with Marisol Arantes.

She wore an odd mix of clothing, the silk dress from the night before and the paint-stained T-shirt he'd found her in the morning they'd first been intimate. When he tried to take them off, she pushed his hands away and Ian decided maybe there was something wrong.

Last night, she'd responded without hesitation or inhibition, but now she seemed to be a bundle of jittery nerves. Was this just a passing mood or was he supposed to read more into it? "Do you want me?" he asked, his mouth trailing down to the soft spot at the base of her neck.

She ran her fingers through his hair. "Oh, yes."

"Then say it," he demanded.

"I want you. I do. It's just—"

"What?"

"There's someone here."

The words hit him like a punch to the stomach. Someone? Another man? Was that why she was so edgy? He drew back and looked down into her eyes. "Right," he murmured, nodding his head. "I'm sorry. I should have called first."

"No, it's not another man. It's Sascha. You met her at the party last night. She's upstairs. We've been… working."

He scolded himself for jumping to conclusions, angry that he'd even allowed a bit of jealousy to creep in. Hell, this wasn't supposed to get so serious, so fast. He glanced over at the door, suddenly anxious to leave. "Ah, business. Well, I'd better let you go then." He kissed her forehead, then picked up the bag and placed it in her arms. "Eat something. And then get some sleep. I'll see you…when I see you."

"Yes," Marisol murmured. "Me, too."

Ian walked to the door and pulled it open, then took one last look at her.

"You're still going to pose for me, aren't you?" she asked.

"Call me," he said.

The door closed behind him and Ian drew a deep breath, then slowly let it out. What the hell was going on? He'd never in his life had that kind of reaction, that immediate rush of jealousy. He barely knew Marisol Arantes and he was worried about the other men who might be interested in her. This was getting out of hand fast and the only way to stop it was to put some distance between the two of them.

Ian grabbed his cell phone from his pocket and hit the speed dial for Marcus, hoping that his brother would be free. He needed to enjoy a few beers with a dispassionate buddy. If his younger brother couldn't snap Ian back to reality, then no one could.

Marcus didn't pick up, but Ian left a message on his voice mail, then headed back to the station. He'd finish the paperwork waiting on his desk and hopefully, by the time he was ready to head home, he'd hear from Marcus.

Anything to take my mind off Marisol, he mused as he drove toward the station. After all they'd experienced together, it was odd that a tiny sliver of jealousy had struck him so hard. But then, she could have been with another man. Marisol was a very sexual woman, a woman who acted on her desires. How did he know there wasn't another man who might be better at satisfying those desires than he was?

When he pulled the squad car into the station parking lot five minutes later, he noticed his brother's truck parked out front. Ian hopped out of the Mustang and strode inside. Marcus was chatting with Sally at the front desk, deep into a discussion of hull design and sail dimensions.

"I was just going to call you," Sally said. "Your brother is here."

"I can see that." Ian beckoned for Marcus to follow him back to his office. Marcus, dressed in a faded T-shirt and baggy shorts, flopped down in the guest chair and idly began to flip through a copy of *Law Enforcement Monthly*.

"I just left a message on your cell," Ian said.

"I know. I was talking with my new boss, Trevor Ross, and couldn't put him on hold. I figured I'd come over here and see you since I thought we might go out for a pint or two."

"So, how's it been going, baby brother?" Ian asked.

"I've been living like a monk, if that's what you're asking. I'm moving out to the boat tomorrow. How are you doing?"

"Great," Ian said. In truth, he felt as if everything he'd enjoyed over the past few days had suddenly gone bad. What had begun as a simple sexual relationship, had grown more serious than he was willing to admit. He considered Marisol his, exclusively, though nothing had been decided between them.

"No women?" Marcus asked.

"I plan to win this bet. Piece of cake." Ian didn't like lying to his brother, but better to keep him in the dark for now. The whole pact had been a ridiculous idea from the start, so if he accidentally broke it, his brothers would have to understand. Having sex with Marisol hadn't really been an accident. It had been a premeditated act of desire, one that he'd thought about from the very moment he'd met her.

"I've been thinking this probably isn't going to work," Ian said. "How are we supposed to learn anything about women if we stay away from them?"

"Celibacy is supposed to give us perspective," Marcus said, peering over the top of the magazine.

"Why do I need that?"

"Maybe you'll figure out why you behave the way you do around women?"

"But what if the perfect woman came along and everything was just right and I knew she was the one. And then, I had this stupid pact to think about. Would you pass up your one chance at a woman like that?"

Marcus thought about his answer for a long time, then shrugged. "How would you know she was perfect? Are you talking about someone who is really hot? Or someone you'd want to spend the rest of your life with?"

"Both," Ian said. "Hypothetically. I mean, would you walk away from someone like that?"

Marcus sat up and tossed the magazine aside. "I don't know. I suppose if I really believed she was the one, then you and Dec would understand. And what's the point of letting the right one get away just because of some silly pact. It defeats the purpose, don't you think?"

"Exactly," Ian said.

Marcus nodded. "But you haven't met the one yet, have you?"

"No. I just met this woman the other day and got to thinking. She was pretty enough, but I met her on the job and—"

"No mixing business with pleasure?" Marcus asked.

A long silence grew between them, both of them deep in thought. At least Marcus would understand Ian's choice. And Declan wasn't the kind of guy who'd begrudge any family member a bit of happiness. Ian glanced over at his brother as he considered telling him the truth about the past few days.

But instead, Ian decided to bring up a different subject. "Have you ever been jealous?"

Marcus frowned. "Of what?"

"Jealous. Of another guy."

"I was wicked jealous of Steve Fillinger after he got that Corvette for high school graduation. I remember telling him the year before, when we got our driver's licenses, that it was my dream car and he convinced his da to buy it for him just to piss me off."

"That's not really jealousy," Ian said. "That's envy. I'm talking about when a woman you're with shows an interest in another man."

Marcus shook his head. "Not really. I guess I've never really cared about someone enough that it bothered me."

"Me, neither," Ian said.

So did that mean that he was beginning to care for Marisol? Even now, he recalled the fierce reaction he'd had when he suspected she was entertaining another man. Was it because he was afraid of losing her for good, or simply losing her for that night? He'd gone over there hoping for a repeat of their previous encounter but would have been satisfied to spend a few hours talking to her. But then, suddenly, everything had become more complicated.

He wanted to discuss it all with his brother, but though they often talked about women, they'd never really discussed the frustrations of trying to navigate a real relationship. Probably because neither one of them had ever had one. Ian was in strange, new territory here and he didn't like how it felt.

Marcus stood and stretched his arms over his head. "Let's go get ourselves a pint and drown our sorrows."

Ian nodded. A pint or two sounded just fine to him. But he wasn't sure he had any sorrows to drown just yet. He wouldn't know that until the next time he saw Marisol Arantes.

4

MARISOL SNATCHED the jar of chocolate sauce from the shelf and distractedly read the calorie content, sighing softly. Nearby, another shopper studied the label on a bag of marshmallows. At 11:00 p.m. on a Friday night, they were a sorry bunch of souls, alone on a perfectly good date night, resigned to eating through whatever cravings they might have.

Her mind contemplated the uses for chocolate sauce and immediately bypassed ice-cream sundaes and settled on the sexual options. She lapsed into a fantasy in which she poured chocolate all over Ian's body and then licked it off. But then, chocolate sauce would be so filling. Perhaps, whipped cream would be a better choice.

Marisol tossed the sauce into her cart, frustrated by her inability to decide what she really wanted—beyond sex. She'd already concluded there were no foods that could serve as a substitute, or even come in a close second. Butter pecan ice cream, Oreo cookies, barbecue potato chips might soothe the hunger, but never really get rid of it.

It had been three days since she'd last seen Ian. She remembered his parting words—call me. And though she'd been expected to make the next move, she'd been reluctant to do so. Sascha had been right. After what she'd discovered in the crate sent by her father, the last person she ought to be sleeping with was a police officer.

Still, her decision to avoid him hadn't diminished her desire for Ian. She'd been edgy and restless, unable to focus on her work and constantly replaying the moments they'd spent together. Everything she started had been left half-finished and Marisol was growing increasingly confused about her feelings for the town's police chief.

She hadn't come to Bonnett Harbor looking to jump into a wildly satisfying sexual affair—she'd come here to work. The affair had just happened and for her part, she'd been glad for it. But now that she'd put a stop to it, Marisol realized she'd begun to need Ian for more than just sex.

As she strolled through the snack aisle again, Marisol looked over her shoulder and noticed someone following her. He'd been behind her for some time, a middle-aged man in a nice suit and undone tie, mildly attractive, yet definitely not her type. Divorced, Marisol calculated, and searching for love at the supermarket. Or maybe just a simple one-night stand.

Ian hadn't been her type, either, far from it. If she'd met him at any other time in her life she might have rejected him, as well, might never have experienced his touch or his taste, the sound of his voice or the scent of his skin.

Marisol continued her aimless stroll, heading toward the freezer section in search of her favorite banana cake.

She turned the corner onto the dairy aisle, suddenly craving onion dip, then froze. Her cart slid to a stop in front of the cream cheese. Ian stood ten feet away, perusing the yogurt selections. She glanced back over her shoulder, wondering if she might be able to turn around without being noticed, but when Marisol looked up again, she caught him staring at her.

He wasn't wearing his uniform. Instead, he was dressed in a faded T-shirt that advertised some fishing service, baggy shorts that hung down nearly to his knees and battered flip-flops. His hair, usually so neatly combed, looked carelessly rumpled. Marisol took in the paint-stained sundress that she'd chosen, smoothing her hands over the wrinkled skirt. Drawing a deep breath, she started toward him, prepared to nod and pass him by if he didn't say anything to her.

For a long moment, he just watched her with an un-readable expression, a carton of yogurt clutched in his hand. Then, Ian stepped out from behind the cart, dropped the yogurt on the floor and walked over to her. In one easy movement, he captured her face in his hands and kissed her, his tongue immediately invading her mouth.

Marisol was so surprised that she didn't have time to react. The contact sent a shock wave through her dulled senses, but then came that wonderful rush of heat that his touch always brought. Her knees wobbled and he caught her around the waist to steady them both. Slowly, the ache that had settled into her body since the last time he'd touched her began to abate and she sank against him.

"That's better," he murmured when he finally drew away. He pressed his forehead to hers and looked down into her eyes. "I've been thinking about you all week."

"I—I've been thinking about you," she admitted. She didn't really want him to know that he'd plagued her thoughts, but what harm could it do. They'd both been honest about their desires.

"I've wanted to—"

She placed her finger on his lips. "I've wanted to call you, too, but I—"

"I wasn't sure you'd want to—" He paused. "Maybe we should stop with the excuses now? So, what are you doing here?"

"Getting something for supper."

He glanced in her basket, then frowned. "And what are you planning to make?"

Marisol smiled wanly at the collection of junk food in her basket. "It's an old Portuguese dish passed down from my grandmother."

He took her hand and pressed a kiss onto the inside of her wrist, his lips lingering over her pulse point. "Come on, leave the groceries. I'll take you out for the best steak on this side of Narragansett Bay."

Marisol grabbed her purse and followed him out of the store. They passed the man in the suit and he gaped at her, obviously thinking that he ought to have introduced himself sooner.

Ian's car was parked on the opposite side of the lot and Marisol wondered if their meeting had been fate. In the end, she really didn't care. She and Ian were together again and nothing else mattered beyond this burning desire she had for the man.

When they reached the car, Ian grabbed her again and kissed her, his fingers furrowing through her hair as he molded his mouth to hers. She felt the possibilities in his kiss, the certainty that, once alone, kissing would never be enough.

She opened to him, her tongue teasing at his in a silent assurance that they both wanted the same thing. The taste of him was like a narcotic, erasing her worries and doubts. She needed Ian in her life, regardless of the risks. And maybe it was just for physical release, but why should that make a difference? If he wanted her and she wanted him, then they could come to some understanding.

"You're hungry?" he asked, his words tinged with another meaning.

She nodded. "Starved."

Ian grinned then took her hand and helped her into his car. As they pulled out of the lot, Marisol tipped her head back and closed her eyes, letting the warm night breeze caress her face, suddenly anxious to rid herself of her clothes.

They only drove for a few minutes before Ian pulled into the driveway of a pretty clapboard bungalow on a tree-lined street. She glanced around. "Where are we?"

"My place," he said.

Marisol glanced over at the house and then at him. They'd always indulged on her turf, on her terms, not on his. She had invited him into her life, for her own purposes, but this was different. He was inviting her into his life now. She sent him an uneasy smile. "I—I thought we were going to go get a—"

"I make a mean steak," he explained as he hopped out of the car. He circled to her door, then opened it and helped Marisol out. He held her hand as they walked up the front steps to the door, then opened it and steered her inside.

The living room was furnished beautifully in an arts and crafts style, with Stickley-inspired furniture throughout. She walked over to a chair and ran her hand along the cherry finish.

"My brother Marcus and I made the furniture," Ian said. "He's kind of an expert with wood."

One side of the room was lined with bookshelves and they were filled from top to bottom. Marisol crossed the room and studied the titles, surprised at the variety. There were classics and contemporary fiction, how-to books and biographies. "Have you read all these?"

Ian nodded. "Would you like something to drink? A glass of wine?"

"That would be nice."

He disappeared into the kitchen and Marisol continued her study of her surroundings. As she looked at the bits and pieces of his life, she realized she didn't know Ian Quinn at all. They'd shared the most intimate of experiences, yet they were little more than strangers. He returned a few moments later with a bottle and a glass. But instead of pouring her a drink, Ian took her hand and pulled her along with him up the stairs.

At first, Marisol thought they might end up in the bedroom, but to her surprise, he took her to the bathroom.

"What are you doing?" she asked, wondering if he was about to repeat what they'd shared in the Templetons' powder room.

"I'm drawing you a bath. It's about time someone took care of you." As he bent over the huge claw-foot tub, her eyes fixed on his shoulders, the muscles moving beneath the T-shirt. A lock of dark hair hung over his collar and she reached out to brush it aside with her fingers. He glanced up at her and smiled as the hot water poured into the tub.

No one had ever taken care of her before, she mused. But it seemed to come so naturally to him, as if he'd accepted the responsibility without a second thought and was happy for it. Ian held up a bottle of bath salts and she nodded.

The scent of rosemary filled the air and bubbles floated on the surface of the water. "I wouldn't think you were the type to take bubble baths," she said, kneeling down beside him to swirl her hand through the water.

"My sister gave me these for Christmas last year. She's into aromatherapy." He leaned against the edge of the tub, his gaze skimming over her face. Then he suddenly stood and pulled her to her feet, his hands sliding down along her arms then lower, to the hem of her sundress. Marisol held her breath as he drew it up over her head.

His gaze raked along the length of her naked body and he laughed softly. "Forgot the underwear again, huh?"

"Yes," she murmured, watching him watch her. She liked how it made her feel when he couldn't keep his eyes off her, the little shiver of anticipation that ran through her. He wanted to touch her; she could see it in the way his fingers twitched. But he was doing his best to resist for now.

Marisol reached for his T-shirt but he gently took her hands and kissed them both. "Why don't you relax? I'll go start dinner." Taking her elbow, he helped her into the tub, then handed her a sponge.

Marisol sank down into the warm water, sighing as she slipped beneath the surface. The scent of the bath salts filled her head and she closed her eyes and lay back, smiling to herself. How was it that he knew exactly what she needed? She hadn't realized how tense she was until the warm water surrounded her.

Marisol opened one eye and found him still staring at her, his gaze lazily focused on her breasts. "Are you sure you don't want to join me?" She held out her hand, beckoning him to come closer, inviting him to touch her. "It's just a bath. And we have been naked before. Or almost naked."

"I thought, after the last time we spoke, you wanted to slow things down."

"It's just a bath," she repeated. But they both knew where it would lead.

"I don't think it would be just a bath, Marisol." He paused and shook his head, sending her a reluctant smile. Then he grabbed the hem of his T-shirt and pulled it off. Ian knelt next to the tub and took the sponge from her hand, then slowly ran it over her breasts. She reached out and drew a damp finger along his chest.

He did have the most incredible body, long limbed

and lean, yet muscled in all the right places. There was a perfection about him that she'd never seen in another man, every part of him in balance, from his broad shoulders to his flat belly and narrow hips, and his long legs.

"That feels nice," she murmured. Marisol leaned back and closed her eyes. She felt his lips on her breasts and she moaned softly. He kissed the curve of her neck. "I've missed you," he said.

A tiny thrill raced through her and she opened her eyes. "You've missed me? Or the sex?"

"You," Ian said as if insulted by her insinuation. He chuckled. "And the sex, a little bit."

Marisol's eyebrow shot up.

"All right, a lot." He ran the sponge along her arms. "Funny. I can't really remember why we decided not to see each other."

"You said you'd call me and you didn't," Marisol said.

"No, I think you said *you'd* call *me*."

In truth, she knew exactly why she hadn't called him. And the reason was now hidden in the back of a storage room in her apartment. For almost a week, she'd been trying to contact her father about that damned painting, but it was as if Hector Arantes had dropped off the face of the planet. She'd left messages with his landlady, who had assured Marisol that her father was well. But that didn't go very far to explain why he'd suddenly disappeared.

The more time that passed, the more Marisol thought she might have overreacted to the whole mess. After all, Ian wasn't about to come banging down her door with a search warrant and a reason to arrest her. He knew nothing about her father and she wasn't about to enlighten him. There were secrets in her life she wasn't required to tell a lover—or even the man she loved.

"How is your work coming?" he asked, drawing the sponge over her shoulder, then following it with his mouth.

"Not well," she said, enjoying the soft caress of his lips on her skin. "I've lost my momentum. I'm going to put off the opening for a few more weeks. I need one important piece and I don't have it."

"Is there something I can do?" he asked.

Marisol turned, stretching her arms along the edge of the tub. "You can make love to me," she whispered, running her hand over his cheek. "That always helps."

His gaze flickered, and for an instant, she thought he might refuse. "Is that all you want from me?" he asked, a sober expression clouding his face.

"What do you mean?"

He paused, as if he were carefully measuring his reply. Then Ian smiled. "Nothing," he murmured. He bent closer and kissed her, his lips soft against hers, his tongue tracing the crease of her mouth.

Marisol smoothed her hands over his chest, the warm water of the bath heightening her sense of touch. Ian slipped his hands beneath her arms and pulled her up until she knelt in the tub. Slowly, he soaked the sponge and then squeezed water over her body, watching as it ran along her skin and between her breasts. Then, he leaned forward and captured her nipple between his lips, sucking gently until he brought it to a tight peak.

Marisol inhaled slowly and tipped her head back,

a wonderful shudder running through her body. Her skin prickled with goose bumps as the air dried it, but she wasn't cold. She reached down and ran her hand over the crotch of his shorts, his shaft growing hard at her touch.

She wanted to feel him inside her again. It would be so easy to crawl out of the tub and push him back on the floor, to sink down on top of him until he filled her completely. But when she moved to do just that, Ian sat back on his heels, his hand resting on his thighs.

"I think I'd better leave you to your bath," he murmured. "I'll go get supper started. You relax." He grabbed the bottle of wine and poured her a glass, then set them both beside the tub.

A moment later, he was gone. Marisol stared at the door for a long time, trying to understand what had just happened. Until now, she'd been able to read Ian's responses quite well. He'd always wanted her as much as she wanted him. Had something changed for him over the past few days? Had his desire ebbed?

She sank down in the water until it reached her nose, her hair floating up around her. This was not the way she'd anticipated the evening would go. But then, nothing had gone as planned from the moment she arrived in Bonnett Harbor.

IAN POKED AT THE CHARCOAL with an old spatula, sparks drifting up into the night air. He took a sip of his beer, then glanced over his shoulder at the light coming from the bathroom window. By all rights, he should be up there now, making love to Marisol. But from the moment he first saw her in the grocery store, his need was tempered by an odd new reality.

This wasn't just about sex anymore. When he saw her, he felt more than just a physical reaction. He was genuinely happy to hear her voice and to see her smile. He found himself wanting to sit with her and talk, to learn more about the woman he knew so well, yet barely knew at all.

But the prospect of feeling something deeper for Marisol frightened the hell out of him. He'd never had a real relationship and wasn't even sure what was expected of him. Suddenly, this affair was moving far too fast and he felt it was about to careen out of control.

Ian heard the back screen door slam and he waited. Marisol probably wasn't aware what it had cost him to walk out of the bathroom and walk away from her. But he'd never cared about the women he'd been with in the past, not beyond the momentary pleasures they might have offered.

He slowly turned and watched her approach. Her hair was wet, the ends making damp streaks on his flannel robe. He thought about the body beneath the faded fabric, the body he'd grown to crave, and realized he liked her dressed in his clothes, bathing in his bathtub, walking through his house. "Are you hungry?" he asked.

She nodded and watched him as he tended the fire. "If you—" Marisol paused and took a deep breath. "If you don't want me anymore you can just tell me. I'll understand."

Ian turned to stare at her, stunned by her statement. Was that what she thought? God, how could she ever believe that, especially after what they'd shared together? Ian doubted that he would ever stop craving her body.

"It's all right," Marisol said. "We both knew what we were getting into when we started this. And it was fun. But I really don't want any messy endings. So please, just be honest."

"You want the truth?" Ian asked.

She sent him a sideways glance, then looked back down into the fire. Her head bobbed in a reluctant nod.

Ian tossed aside the spatula and took her face in his hands, kissing her thoroughly. A tiny cry of surprise slipped from her lips, but then she gave herself over to him, opening her mouth and tasting him fully. He undid the tie on the robe and brushed aside the soft fabric, running his hands over her naked skin.

When he drew back, her lips were damp and her eyes half-shuttered. "My problem is that I want you too much," he murmured. "Every second of my day is spent wondering when I'm going to be with you again and how it's going to be between us. Does that scare you, Marisol? Because it sure as hell scares me."

She laughed softly, her fingertips coming up to his face to touch his smile. "I'm not afraid," she said.

"Then maybe I shouldn't be, either." Ian smoothed her damp hair back from her face and looked deeply into her dark eyes. How the hell was he supposed to know where this was going? And did it make any difference? He'd always imagined that falling in love was a leap of faith. Everyone knew the odds were fifty-fifty at best.

Throwing himself into a full-fledged love affair with Marisol Arantes was just as hazardous. This wasn't a series of one-night stands for him. He wanted more, something concrete, defined. But what? Until he knew for sure, perhaps it was best to keep his real fears to himself.

"Sometimes I wonder if I can get through the day without kissing you or touching you or…or having you inside of me," she said. "But there's nothing wrong with wanting each other. It's perfectly natural."

His hands skimmed over her body, smoothing over the soft curves of her hips and buttocks. "Obsession is natural?"

"Are you obsessed?" she asked.

"It feels that way," Ian admitted, as he pulled her against his body. "Hell, I've arrested guys for stalking and wondered how they could be so stupid, so weak. These last few days, I've had to fight the temptation to drive by the gallery, to knock on your door and see if you're there, just for a chance to seduce you all over again."

"Then do it," Marisol challenged. "Seduce me."

"No," Ian said.

"No?"

He ran his thumb over her lower lip. "Not until you tell me three things about yourself that I don't know."

Marisol frowned. "Why?"

"Humor me," he said.

"All right. But if I confess three things, then you have to confess three things, as well."

"You start," Ian said.

She thought for a long moment, then smiled. "I hate being tickled. That's one." She paused. "My favorite spot on a man's body is that little indentation at the base of his spine. And…I like it when you whisper in my ear when you're moving inside of me."

His brow arched. "I thought maybe you might tell me your favorite color or your birthday or where you grew up. But I guess that will have to do for now."

"Now you," Marisol said. "And I don't care about your birthday or your favorite color. I want to know intimate things."

"I don't like eggs for breakfast," Ian began. "And I like it when you don't wear underwear and I'm the only one who knows. And I love the way your hair brushes against my chest when you're on top of me."

She smiled. "And I like it when I first touch you, when I wrap my fingers around you and you stop breathing for a second." Marisol reached out and slowly unbuttoned his jeans, then touched him.

Ian growled softly. "I like that, too."

"Are you happy? Do you know everything you need to know?"

"It's a start," he said.

"Now will you seduce me?" Marisol asked.

Ian glanced around, then took her hand and led her to a hammock in a secluded corner of the yard. The high fence shielded them from the view of nosy neighbors and an old apple tree provided shadows in which to disappear. He helped her into the hammock, waiting until she was stretched out before he lay down behind her, cradling her body against his.

Ian ran his hands over her, touching her through the thin flannel. Slowly, he drew the robe up along her thighs and hips until he could slip his hands between her legs. His fingers brushed the tiny triangle of hair before slipping into the warm, damp slit beyond. When he touched her, her body belonged to him. He was the only one who could make her shudder with ecstasy.

Marisol moaned softly as Ian began to stroke her, back and forth in a gentle rhythm that made her writhe in his arms. Almost immediately, he saw the signs she was close to the edge and he slowed his tempo, willing to wait as long as he could.

She reached around to touch him, but his jeans got in the way. Ian took care of that with his free hand, releasing himself as he shoved the jeans and boxers down.

Marisol rubbed back against him and when she felt the heat of his erection on her skin, she shifted until he was pressed between the soft curves of her backside. Gently, she took him in hand and guided him between her legs. And then, suddenly, he was inside her.

Ian sucked in a sharp breath, the instinct to move almost overwhelming him. He knew he ought to use a condom, but the feeling of her body surrounding him, hot and damp and tight, was too perfect to resist. He slowly pushed forward, then drew back, knowing he was tempting fate.

"Don't move," he said, knowing it wouldn't take much for him to come.

"I have to move," Marisol replied. "It's all right."

He pressed a kiss into the curve of her neck. "Is it?" She nodded, reaching back to run her hands through his hair. Usually, Ian would never take the chance, knowing what an unplanned pregnancy could do to a guy's life. "No babies?"

"No," she said, moving against him. "That's covered. And so are the other things."

He'd never had sex without a condom, yet had always wondered what it would feel like, to touch a woman in the most intimate way, to leave part of himself inside her body. He slowly began to move again, indescribable sensations coursing through him as he sheathed himself in her heat.

The hammock pressed their bodies together and he could barely move his hips, but it was enough to bring him right to the edge. He reached around her and continued to caress her clitoris.

Ian nuzzled her ear. "You feel so good," he murmured, his voice ragged.

She moaned softly and arched against him, her fingers tangling in his hair. He never changed his pace, but instead drove deeper with each stroke, withdrawing even more slowly. She whispered his name and the pressure to surrender grew inside him. Every movement sent a frisson of desire racing through his body, setting his nerves on fire until he knew he'd die if he didn't come soon.

And when he felt her tense in his arms, he drew back

and drove deep. The orgasm hit her hard and she cried out, her voice echoing in the night air. And then, buried inside her, he came, spasms of pleasure shooting through him.

Slowly, Ian began to move again, taking the last of his orgasm to bring her down from hers. But he continued on, long after they were both spent. To his surprise, he stayed hard and within minutes, brought her to another orgasm.

They lay snuggled in the hammock, Ian's arms wrapped around her, their legs tangled together. "Even now, I want you again," he murmured, trailing kisses along her shoulder.

"I don't think it will ever be enough," she said, turning so that he might kiss her mouth.

"I hope not," Ian replied. He caught her lower lip between his teeth and bit gently. "I hope it's never enough."

THE SHRILL RING of the phone split the silence of the gallery. Marisol wiped the paint off her hands, then strolled to the worktable and grabbed the cordless phone. Ian had promised to call and make plans for dinner for that evening, but it was barely noon.

"Gallerie Luna," she answered. "This is Marisol."

Her father's voice replied. "Mari?"

"Papi? Where are you? I've been trying to get hold of you for a week now!"

"I'm here, in this town of yours."

"Don't come here," Marisol warned. "Not now. Tell me where you are and I'll meet you."

"There is a rest stop on the highway just north of town. Meet me there," he said.

The line clicked dead and she stared at the phone for a moment, then dropped it on the table. Grabbing her car keys, Marisol raced to the door, then paused, tempted to get the painting and give it back to him. Her mother had begged her the first time her father had been in trouble to distance herself, but Marisol had stuck by him. She had more to lose this time, so much more. Was she willing to risk it for her father?

She locked the gallery door behind her, then hurried to her car, parked halfway down the block. Glancing over her shoulder, she pulled out into traffic, muttering to herself as she drove. As she headed out of town, she ignored the speed limit, deftly avoiding an elderly couple trying cross in front of the post office.

Marisol had spent a week trying to figure out what to do with the painting. If she could only be certain it wouldn't be traced back to her father, then she'd simply drop it off at the front door of the Templetons' Newport mansion. But when it came to art forgery, there would be very few suspects on the short list, a list that would inevitably include her father.

There was nowhere to turn for help. If David was involved, then he'd protect his own interests at all costs. He'd never been the altruistic sort. And she couldn't possibly ask Sascha to endanger her reputation. There was no legal way to get the original back where it belonged, if she indeed had the original.

But there were some illegal ways, she mused. If art could be stolen, then it could be returned just as easily. And if she made friends with Mrs. Templeton, perhaps she'd gain a way inside. Now all she had to do was find a willing art thief who'd do his job in reverse. Perhaps her father could provide a name.

She was only a mile from the rest stop when she glanced in the rearview mirror and saw the police car following her. A sick feeling settled in her stomach and she waited, hoping that the officer was on another errand. But then he turned the lights on and blasted the siren and Marisol had no choice but to pull over.

She waited as the officer got out of the car then let out a tightly held breath when she realized it was Ian. He smiled as he approached, removing his sunglasses and squatting down beside the car. "Hey there," he said. "This is becoming a habit."

"Did I do something wrong, Officer?" Marisol asked, sending him a nervous smile.

"Actually, you did," Ian replied. "You ran the stop sign on Perry Street and Vine. And then you didn't yield to the pedestrians on the next block."

Marisol gasped. "I'm sorry, I didn't even realize." She touched her temple. "I'm a little distracted. Tired, too."

He frowned at her. "Is everything all right?"

"Of course," she said in a cheerful tone. "I just—*we* just didn't sleep much last night and I've been working since early this morning."

Ian grinned. "Well, I guess since I'm the cause of your distraction, I really can't write you up," he said as he stood. "I'll just give you a warning this time, but be more careful. I don't want anything happening to you."

"It won't," she murmured.

He reached out and ran his finger along her bare forearm, his touch sending a shiver through her body. "So, am I going to see you tonight? I have this thing with my brothers, but I can come over later."

She nodded. "Call me."

"I'll do that." Ian turned and headed to the police cruiser. He looked back once and Marisol waved, relief washing over her. This was only going to get more difficult if she didn't find a way to solve her little dilemma. Ian waited until she pulled back into traffic, then followed her for a bit, before he made a U-turn and headed back into town.

As she drove the last mile to the rest stop, Marisol's thoughts returned to the previous night. Every instinct told her she ought to put him out of her life, at least until she got rid of the painting. But it was no use. Her attraction to Ian Quinn was not something she could ignore or resist. Having Ian in her life, in her bed and in her body was the only thing she cared about, and it was worth the risk.

Marisol spotted her father's car before she turned into the rest stop. She pulled into a parking spot about twenty feet away and then walked over to one of the picnic tables set beneath a large maple tree. A few seconds later, her father sat down beside her.

"I know what you are going to say," he muttered, hanging his head. "And you would be right. I let myself get involved in something that might cause us both trouble."

"Papi, why did you send me that painting?"

"I had to get rid of it. I couldn't bear to have it around.

I couldn't even look at it. David said the FBI had come to him with questions about one of his clients. The client who paid for the painting. David has been waiting to smuggle it out of the country in one of his shipments, but it's been too risky."

"Then David is involved. Did he put you up to this?" Marisol asked.

Hector nodded. "I needed the money."

"You could have come to me for help. I would have given you the money."

"After all I have taken from you and your mother, I could not ask," he said.

"And yet, you put me in the middle of this?"

"I didn't know where else to turn. David asked me to hold on to the original. What choice did I have? But I decided I had to make this right. If we can switch the paintings, I can destroy the forgery before anyone finds out. David will be left to deal with his client."

She shook her head, unable to believe that she'd once loved David Barnett. He was nothing more than a common criminal. "Then that is the original Colter."

Hector nodded. "I painted a copy for him when he had the original in his gallery. That's not my painting."

"How did he make the switch without getting caught?"

"Before the sale. He authenticated the painting and he sold it, so there were no questions."

"He knows the Templetons," Marisol said. "They'd be stupid enough to trust him doing both. If there was only a way to get the forgery out of their house. Then we could switch the two and no one would have to know."

"You can find a way. That's why I sent you the painting."

She stood up, her hands clenched at her sides. "I will find a way out of this. And you will find somewhere quiet where you can stay until I do. Don't go back to your place, just keep driving north." Marisol reached in her purse and grabbed her wallet, then pulled out three hundred dollars. "Go up to Maine and visit your old friend Edgar. Tell him you need the peace and quiet so that you can paint again. He'll let you stay at the cabin for a month or two. I'll send you more money once you get there."

Her father stared down at the cash she offered, then reluctantly took it. "All right." He slowly got to his feet and then made an attempt to hug her.

At first, Marisol drew away, but then her emotions overcame her and she threw her arms around his neck. "Go," she said. "And don't let anyone know where you are, not David, not anyone. I'll contact you."

She watched as her father walked toward his car. He seemed so old and frail now, nothing like the man she remembered from her childhood. Life had not been kind to Hector Arantes. He'd given everything to his art and no one had recognized his talent.

Tears pushed at the corners of her eyes and Marisol swallowed them back. How had she been so lucky? Everything had always come so easily to her. From the moment she'd started painting, people had taken notice. And when she'd tried sculpting, her popularity had increased even more. Some collectors could barely wait to see her new work and she'd already had three shows in prominent New York galleries.

But she'd put everything into her work, to the exclusion of a personal life. Even David had been a good business move at the time, although she hadn't seen his true character until it was too late. Her father had tried to make a life for his family. Maybe a successful artist just couldn't have both. Success required a selfishness that was in direct opposition to a happy personal life.

She'd convinced herself of that fact after she'd caught David cheating, finding it a convenient rationalization for her pain and loneliness. But now that she'd met Ian, Marisol had begun to believe that things could be different, that she didn't have to give up everything to enjoy success.

He made her feel anything was possible, as if work and life—and even love—might coexist. She turned and walked to her car, he mind filled with thoughts of him. Suddenly, she needed to know more, all the tiny details of his life, what he loved and what he hated. He'd been right last night. They didn't know each other. There were so many questions yet to ask.

She sped down the highway toward Bonnett Harbor, the morning breeze blowing through her hair, exhaustion suddenly overwhelming her. She hadn't slept much the previous night, making love in Ian's bed until deep into the night before he returned her to the grocery store to pick up her car in the predawn hours.

Once she'd returned to the gallery, she'd jumped right into work without a thought to eating or sleeping. And now, it was catching up with her. But when she pulled up in front of the gallery, she noticed a familiar car parked across the street—a steel-gray Mercedes sedan. She groaned softly as she pulled into a vacant parking spot, then sat behind the wheel and waited.

He came strolling over to the car with his customary swagger, dressed in a finely tailored Prada suit and Italian shoes. There had been a time when his every move had enthralled her, but now she was just angry with him. Marisol pasted a smile on her face. "Hello, David. What are you doing here?"

He stood over her, the sun at his back. She couldn't see his face as she squinted to look up at him. But she knew he was smirking. "It's been awhile," he said, pulling open her car door. "I just thought I'd check in and see how things were going."

"Everything is going just fine," Marisol said as she got out of the car, avoiding the hand that he extended to help her. They both stood on the street, Marisol's anger simmering.

"Your father has been keeping me up-to-date with what you've been doing," he said. "But I haven't talked to him in a few weeks. I thought maybe he was up here visiting."

Marisol knew immediately what he'd come for. He needed his painting and he couldn't find it. But he didn't know she had it. "Don't lie to me. I know what you're here for." She drew back and slapped him across the face, his head snapping to the side with the force of her blow. "That's for the Brazilian bimbo in my bed. And no, there's no chance that I would ever want you back in my life. So turn around and go back to New York."

David's friendly expression instantly turned hard. "You might not want to be so quick to judge me."

"No?" she asked. "I've had six months to judge you, David, and I'm afraid you've come off looking like the biggest ass on the East Coast."

He chuckled, the sound grating on her nerves. "I'm in town to see the Templetons, but I'm not due there until dinner. I've taken a room over in Newport. I thought I'd check out some of the other galleries in my spare time, look around for some promising new artists. I could use a tour guide."

Marisol took care not to react when he mentioned the Templetons. Was he planning to steal the forgery and sell that to his client? If he was, then David had to be desperate. "I'm busy. I'll be busy for the rest of the year. In other words, I really don't want to spend any time with you, David. We have nothing more to say to each other." She walked toward the front door of the gallery.

"Marisol, I know things didn't end—"

"Stop!" she snapped, turning on him. "Nothing you have to say to me will make me change my mind about you. Go away, David, and leave me alone."

She hurried to the door and unlocked it, then slipped inside. With a sigh, Marisol slid down to the floor and wrapped her arms around her knees, her back braced against the entryway wall.

She closed her eyes and wished that Ian were with her, to soothe her frayed nerves and to distract her thoughts, to make her feel safe and protected. But this was her problem to deal with, and unless she could solve it, there would be no Ian. If things fell to pieces, he would be coming to her door with his handcuffs— to arrest her.

5

THE PUB WAS PACKED, the Saturday-night crowd gathered around the bar to watch a Red Sox game. Ian grabbed a pitcher of beer from the bartender and headed to the pool table, set in an alcove near the back of the bar. Marcus and Declan were caught up in a game of pool with two of the regulars and Ian set the beer on a nearby table then found a seat on an empty stool.

He glanced at his watch as he'd done so many times over the past hour. He'd promised Marisol he'd call her before he came over, but if he waited too long, it might seem more like a booty call than a genuine desire to be with her.

He and Dec and Marcus had been forced to cancel their regular Friday night out last night because Dec had a security job scheduled, so they'd agreed to meet at Finnerty's on Saturday.

A few weeks ago, Ian would have looked forward to a night out with his brothers. But now that Marisol had entered his life, he'd lost all interest in hanging out, in playing pool or darts or in trying to analyze the female sex over a pitcher of beer. From the moment he'd first touched Marisol, Ian couldn't explain why he wanted her. He didn't care why. His affair with Marisol was exciting and unpredictable and confusing. Trying to figure it all out would only make it seem ordinary.

Marcus sank the eight ball in the corner pocket, ending the game, then held out the cue to Ian. Ian shook his head. "I'm done."

Marcus glanced at Dec and they turned the table over to the next pair of players. He sat down next to Ian and sipped at his beer, watching as the players racked the balls. Dec returned the cues and wandered over to his brothers. A pretty blonde stopped him, her hand coming to rest on his arm. He bent close to listen to what she said, then nodded and grinned, before she joined her friends at a nearby booth.

"You're never going to last," Ian warned as Dec found another stool.

"Just because I converse with a woman does not mean I feel compelled to sleep with her. She asked if I wanted to play a game of pool and I said no, that I had to leave soon." He took a long drink of his beer. "So what's the topic of conversation for tonight?"

"Jealousy," Marcus suggested. "Ian and I were talking about that the other night."

Ian shot his brother an irritated look, but Dec seemed to find the topic intriguing. "Who are you jealous of?" he asked.

"No one," Ian said. "It was just hypothetical."

"Tell him about your other hypothetical," Marcus urged. "The one where you meet the girl of your dreams and you have to break the pact."

Ian knew that Marcus was goading him on, but he wasn't going to take the bait. "Hey, I was just wondering what would happen. Let's be real. Which one of us is going to turn a woman down because of this silly deal we made?"

"I would," Marcus said, raising his hand.

"That's because you've got no game in the first place," Dec teased. "But, I'd turn a woman down, for the greater good."

"We swore on the medallion," Marcus said. "We can't break the pact."

"Even if you met some nymphomaniac swimsuit model who was going back to Australia tomorrow? You wouldn't sleep with her?" Ian asked.

His brothers shook their heads.

"Bollocks," Ian said. "You are both bleedin' liars."

"We swore on the medallion," Dec said. "You can't break a promise like that. You'd probably be cursed." He studied Ian's expression. "Or did you already break the pact?"

Ian stood. "I have to go. I've got to work tomorrow at the fire department picnic." *Now who was the liar,* Ian mused. He'd pawned that job off on Delaney and Wilson.

"I'm gonna stay," Marcus said. "Maybe win some more money at pool. These guys can't play worth shite."

Dec clapped Ian on the shoulder. "I'll walk you out. I've got a presentation in Manhattan tomorrow morning and I need to drive down there tonight. I'm doing background checks for a company down there."

They wove their way through the crowd in the bar

and when they reached the street, Ian stopped. "So what do you find out in these background checks?"

"Pretty much the same thing law enforcement has. But we also check into personal history. Employment, marriages, boyfriends and girlfriends. Even schooling."

"Answers to all the questions," Ian murmured.

"All the important questions," Dec replied.

"Could you do a check for me?" The moment Ian made the request, he wanted to take it back. Sure, he'd been curious about Marisol's past. It was in his nature to be cautious. And if he was going to fall in love with her, he deserved to know a little more about her. But still, it seemed a bit underhanded to use his connections to learn more.

"What's the name?"

Ian paused, then brushed aside his qualms. What would the report say? Not much more than he already knew. So it really wasn't a big deal. After all, it wasn't as though he expected to find a string of arrests and a prison record. "Her name is Marisol Arantes. She's from New York and she drives a Triumph Spitfire and she's an artist who just moved into town. That's about all I know about her."

He wasn't about to tell his brother about Marisol's beautiful body or about the way her hair felt when he ran his fingers through it or about how her face flushed in the moments before she came. Ian knew those details, but not a whole lot more.

"And why do you want to know about her?" Declan asked.

"Curiosity. That's not breaking the deal we made, is it?"

"Depends on how far you take your curiosity," Dec said. He considered the request, then nodded. "Hell, if it will win me the money, I'll get you anything you want. I'll put someone on it right away. I should have something for you by Tuesday." He gave Ian a playful punch to the shoulder. "Maybe I should encourage this?"

"Piss off," Ian muttered, a sarcastic edge to his words. He watched as Dec headed off to his car, then glanced at his watch again. It was nearly ten, but Marisol usually worked late into the night. Maybe she was ready for a break.

He'd grown a bit protective of Marisol as of late. She didn't seem to take care of herself when she was working. She rarely bothered to eat or to sleep, and often, she looked as if she were on the edge of exhaustion. He didn't always understand her art, but he did know how to make her life a bit easier.

Bonnett Harbor's favorite ice-cream stand was still open and Ian left Finnerty's and drove down to the waterfront, intent on getting something to tempt her away from work. He ordered a raspberry sundae at the drive-through. Maybe he did know more about her than he realized. From what she'd had in her cart at the grocery store the other night, he knew she liked junk food, anything sweet and anything crunchy.

A tiny sliver of guilt shot through him as he turned the Mustang onto Bay Street. So why the hell did he need a background check? What could it tell him that would make any difference? Would he want her any less if she'd passed a bad check or been fired from a job?

As Ian drove by Gallerie Luna, searching for a place to park, he noticed two things—the lights were off inside the gallery and a shadowy figure stood in the doorway, bent over the lock. He pulled the car around the block, then hopped out, leaving the sundae sitting on the front seat. He wasn't carrying his gun, but he did have a night-stick and a pair of cuffs in the trunk. He grabbed them both, along with his radio. Then, keeping close to the storefronts, made his way down to Marisol's place.

The streets were eerily quiet. Usually there were at least a few pedestrians out at ten o'clock on a summer night, people walking their dogs, diners heading home from the local restaurants. When he got within fifteen feet of the gallery, he could tell the figure was a man and that he was working at the lock with a small tool.

Ian took a deep breath and settled on a strategy. He'd whack the guy on the knee, then grab his arms and cuff him before he had a chance to turn around. But just as Ian came close enough to touch him, the intruder managed to get the door open.

The moment it swung open, an alarm sounded. He spun around, only to find Ian standing in his way. One quick jab in the stomach was enough to double him over. Ian shoved him into the gallery, rolled him over, then put a knee in his back. He grabbed his arms and put on the handcuffs.

"Get up," he growled, yanking him to his feet.

"What the hell are you—get off me!"

Ian grabbed his radio from his jacket pocket, ready to call in for backup, but Marisol suddenly appeared, dressed in a short little nightgown, her hair tumbled around her face.

"What are you doing?" she shouted over the sound of the alarm. She glanced back and forth between the two of them, covering her ears. "David?"

"You know this guy?" Ian yelled.

"Yes," she said, nodding her head. "His name is David Barnett. Why is he in handcuffs?"

"He was trying to break in." Ian winced. "Can you turn off the alarm?"

She disappeared, and a few seconds later, the alarm fell silent. When she returned, she stood in front of them both. "Who's going to start?"

"This idiot just knocked me over and put me in hand-cuffs," Barnett explained. "I was knocking on the door, hoping you were still up and—"

"He was messing with the lock," Ian said. "How do you suppose he got the door open?"

"It was unlocked already," David said.

"Bullshit," Ian replied. "Marisol, did you lock the door?"

"I—I thought I did," she said. A frown wrinkled her brow. "But maybe I didn't." She ran her hand through her rumpled hair. "Just let him go," she finally said.

"I can't do that," Ian replied. "He was trying to break in."

"He wasn't," she said. "I—I asked him to come over and I forgot."

Ian could tell she was lying but he wasn't sure why. With a soft curse, he unlocked the cuffs, leaning forward to whisper in Barnett's ear. "We both know what you were doing," he said. "I'd suggest you get out of town, before I find something else to arrest you for."

Barnett cursed, giving Ian a shove. "Marisol, I—"

Ian went after him, ready to arrest him for assaulting an officer, but Marisol stepped in between them both. "Ian, wait here," she ordered. She pointed to a spot near the door and Ian reluctantly did as he was told.

Then she walked outside, closing the door behind her. But Ian pulled the blinds aside and watched her as she spoke with the guy she called David. They appeared to be more than just passing acquaintances, but it was obvious from the way she was gesturing to him, that they weren't on good terms.

He watched as the skinny strap from her nightgown dropped over her shoulder, revealing the soft flesh of her breast. She angrily pulled it up, but continued talking. He saw Barnett's gaze drop to her breasts and fought back a surge of anger.

When the guy reached out and took Marisol's hand, Ian cursed softly, grabbing the door handle, ready to step between them. He shouldn't feel this way, as if Marisol belonged to him. They'd known each other exactly one week. It wasn't nearly enough time to consider her anything more than an extended one-night stand.

But that wasn't how he felt. In truth, he couldn't recall ever feeling that way about her. From the very start, Ian had sensed that there was something more between them, something holding them together beyond basic lust and desire.

Ian walked away from the door, convincing himself he didn't care who the man was to Marisol, or how she felt about him. For now, Ian was in her life and he wasn't about to be displaced by some smart-ass city boy in a fancy suit. The guy was up to no good, and tomorrow, he'd call his brother and ask him to cancel the background check on Marisol, and instead, concentrate on David Barnett.

MARISOL STEPPED INSIDE the gallery and shut the door behind her, leaning back against it and closing her eyes. She'd planned to spend a quiet evening, catching up on her sleep and trying to put her troubles aside for just a little while. But the longer she had the painting in her possession, the more trouble seemed to find her.

If David had been breaking in, then she knew exactly what he was looking for. He intended to steal the painting from her and sell it to his client. But once the sale was complete, then her father was just as culpable as David— if they got caught. Maybe she ought to just give it to him and be done with it, to take the chance and pray that the odds would be with her and no one would ever find out.

"Is he gone?"

Marisol looked up to see Ian standing in the shadows of the gallery, his frame outlined by the feeble light from the street shining through the transom windows. "Yes. He's gone."

He slowly approached, stopping just far enough away that she couldn't read his expression. "Would you like to explain to me what that was all about?"

She shook her head. "Not now. I'm tired and I want to go back to bed." She walked toward the back of the gallery, then turned. "Are you coming?"

Ian cursed softly. "Who was that guy?"

She didn't care for the tone in his voice, but if answering his questions would get them to bed any faster, then she was willing to do it. "David Barnett. My ex."

"Ex what?" he asked, his voice tense.

"Boyfriend," she said. "Fiancé, actually. We were engaged for about six months."

Ian let the revelation settle for a while before he responded. "How long ago did you break up?"

"Six months," she said. "That's why I decided I needed to get out of the city. To get away from him, to make a fresh start."

"Do you still have a thing for him?"

"Why all the questions?" Marisol snapped. "He's no longer in my life. Isn't that enough?"

He crossed the room, standing silently in front of her, staring down at her face. Then, he grabbed Marisol's hand and drew it to his mouth, kissing the center of her palm. "Am *I* in your life, Marisol?"

She drew a sharp breath, the question taking her by surprise. Was he? Even in the very early days of her relationship with David, she never felt the way she did when she was with Ian. Her heart beat ten times more each minute when Ian touched her and she always seemed to be a little breathless when he was near. And at times, she couldn't think straight.

He wasn't just in her life. He'd carved out a corner

in her heart and stolen a tiny piece of her soul. "Yes," she finally admitted. "I guess you are."

At that, Ian pulled her into his arms and gave her a fierce kiss, his mouth covering hers until she had no choice but surrender. When he finally pulled back, Ian brushed her tousled hair from her eyes and smiled. "I was worried about you. He was breaking in and all I could think about was your safety." He paused and frowned. "Why do you think he was doing that?"

"I don't know that he was breaking in," she lied. "I saw him earlier today and told him I didn't want to talk to him. Maybe he wasn't ready to take no for an answer. And I've been so distracted, I probably did forget to lock the door."

Ian pulled her along to the rear of the gallery, then gently pushed her down on the sofa. He sat beside her, her hands folded in his. "Tell me," he said.

"Why? It's over now."

"Humor me. I want to know who this guy is and what he meant to you."

She sighed. "He's an art dealer in Manhattan. We met at a gallery opening two years ago, we moved in together a year ago, and six months ago, I caught him in our bed with a twenty-one-year-old Brazilian model. I kicked him out, he took his stuff, and I decided to move up here for a while." The story made her sound like a gullible fool, but she knew Ian would side with her and consider David the enemy.

"And that's it? It's over?"

"For me," she said. She stood and pulled him to his feet. "Completely over. Now, are you going to come to bed or are you going to continue to interrogate me? Because, if you're going to continue with the questions, I might have to call a lawyer."

Ian grinned. "You're not under arrest. You don't need a lawyer." He held up his handcuffs. "Unless you want me to put these on you."

She took them from his fingers. "What do I need to do to get you to take your clothes off?"

Ian shrugged. "A kiss might work," he said.

She grabbed his face and pressed her mouth to his, then drew back. "How's that?"

"That'll take care of my shoes." He kicked off his Nikes and reached down to yank off a sock.

Marisol grabbed the front of his shirt and pulled him toward the back of the gallery. When they reached the stairs to her apartment, she stood on the step above him and kissed him again, this time teasing his mouth open with her tongue. For good measure, she dropped a trail of kisses along his jaw to a spot just below his left ear.

Ian growled playfully. "That's worth a sock and my shirt." He pulled off the second sock and by the time he straightened, Marisol was already working on the buttons of his shirt. When she had the first three undone, he grabbed the hem and pulled it over his head, tossing it aside.

"That was easy," she murmured, running her hands over his broad shoulders. "What's it going to take for you to get rid of the pants?"

"Make me an offer," he said.

She slowly pulled him along with her, up the stairs.

When they reached the landing, Marisol pushed him against the wall and pressed her lips to his chest. With her tongue, she traced a path to his nipple, then sucked on it gently until it rose in a hard peak. She drew back and blew on it and Ian groaned.

"The pants?" she asked.

"The belt," he countered.

"And the zipper," she said.

Ian removed his belt, then slowly lowered his zipper. He was already aroused, the little game they played silly, yet sexually charged. "Now what?" he asked.

She stood staring at him, the beauty of his half-naked body capturing her complete attention. Suddenly, her desire to possess him dissolved, replaced by an equally burning need to paint him. Her gaze slid from his face to his chest and then to his belly and back up again. She grabbed him by the hand and started back down the stairs. "Hurry," she murmured, desperate to get her vision down on paper.

Ian held back, pulling her to a stop. "Where are we going?"

"Just come with me," she insisted. She hurried downstairs to the gallery and left him standing near one of the low benches that lined the walls. Flipping on a contractor's light that hung from a cord on one of the pillars, Marisol aimed it at the wall. Then she grabbed her sketch pad and a piece of charcoal and perched on a nearby stool.

"Take the rest off," she ordered, staring down at the blank page and focusing on what she needed to draw.

Ian chuckled. "You're not going to draw me. Come on, Marisol, let's go to bed. You've been working too hard."

Marisol turned and stared at him intently, her gaze skimming over his body from top to toe. Catching her lower lip between her teeth, she circled the charcoal above the paper. "I have to do this now," she murmured. "I have to get it down before I lose it." Tossing the pad and charcoal aside, she walked over to him and finished unzipping his pants, then drew them down to his ankles. His boxers followed.

Though Ian had been naked with her before, undressing him now seemed almost improper. Marisol had leave to take in every detail and what she saw was stunning, masculine beauty that took her breath away.

He reached for his pants, but she shook her head. "Please. It won't take long, I promise. Then we'll go to bed."

Reluctantly, Ian stepped out of his clothes. She walked over to the wall and braced her hands above her head, leaning forward. "Like this," she said. "I want to see the muscles in your back."

Ian did as he was told and Marisol slowly walked around him, running her hands over his body, checking to see how the light and shadows played across his skin. "Relax. Like you're standing in a shower with the water pouring down on you. Lean into the wall and put one foot forward a bit. And let your head drop slightly."

Though she wasn't trying to excite him, she could see what her touch was doing. His shaft was stiff and ready, brushing against his belly. For a moment, she thought about easing his need first and drawing him later. But she cast the notion aside and continued to observe him.

"How long will this—"

"Shh!" she said. "Don't talk."

Marisol grabbed her digital camera from the work-table and began to snap pictures of him, but he turned around and held his hand out.

"What are you doing?"

"It's just to help me remember," she said.

"If those pictures get out, the folks in this town are going to demand my resignation."

She smiled, dropping her gaze to his rigid shaft. "I think they might be impressed rather than upset. Now turn around and let me do this."

Over the next hour, Marisol completed sketch after sketch of Ian, putting him in different poses and adjusting the light until it cast his beautiful body in sharp contrasts. They didn't speak, Ian growing more comfortable with the task at hand and anxious to please her.

Having him pose made the work so simple. They were lovers, so she didn't have to worry about what she asked him to do, or how she touched his body. There had always been rules when she'd worked with nude models, but with Ian, there were no rules.

She glanced up from the sketch pad and took a good look at him. He was lying on one of the low, uphol-stered benches, one leg hanging off the side, the other bent. His head was tipped back, his arm carelessly covering his eyes.

"Can you make yourself hard again?" she asked.

His arm dropped away from his eyes and he turned and looked at her, as if he'd misunderstood. "What?"

"Touch yourself," she said. "I want you to be... aroused."

He smiled. "Why don't you take care of that?"

"I can't," she said. Marisol knew the moment she touched him in that way, she'd forget about her work and begin to obsess about the pleasures that his body offered. Even now, it would be difficult to just sit and watch him touch himself. But for this drawing, she needed to see his desire in order to draw it.

He ran his hand over his chest, then his belly, but he stopped there. She waited. Finally, he closed his eyes and moved lower. Marisol watched as he stroked himself, curious and yet detached. She knew men pleasured themselves on a regular basis, but she'd never actually watched how it was done.

He began slowly, wrapping his fingers around his shaft as she had done for him. It didn't take long before he was hard and he stopped. By that time, she'd lowered her sketch pad, much more interested in watching him.

"Don't stop," she murmured.

He didn't open his eyes, but merely smiled. Marisol set the sketchbook and charcoal down on the floor and slowly crossed to him, her eyes scanning his body, watching for the cues to his desire.

Though he had to know she was near, he continued on, his head tipped back, his lips slightly parted. She reached for the straps of her nightgown, brushing them off her shoulders and letting the loose garment drop to the floor in front of the bench.

Marisol reached out to touch him, but instead, let her hand hover close to his skin, feeling the warmth of his body and listening to his quickened breathing. She bent over him, her hair brushing along his chest, then touched the tip of his penis with her tongue.

Ian moaned softly. She crawled on top of him, and a moment later, he slipped inside her. Only then, did he open his eyes and look at her. Marisol smiled, smoothing her hands over his chest. For a long time, they just stared at each other, unmoving, the silent communication more arousing than any foreplay they had enjoyed.

He reached between them and touched her. Already, he was so familiar with her responses, so attuned to her body and ready to please her. Sex had become something more than just mutual gratification. Between them, it had become an expression of trust and understanding, a refuge from the troubles that invaded her life. She was safe with Ian.

He arched against her and Marisol held her breath. Then, he sat up and grabbed her around the waist, swinging his feet to the floor. She felt him buried so deep inside her it made her ache. Ian looked up at her as she began to rock above him, his gaze taking in every reaction, the need beginning to spiral out of control.

With every moment that she spent with him, this connection grew stronger, like strands being added to a rope. It had grown so quietly and now, Marisol couldn't imagine any other man in her life. Everything that she needed was here. Though she didn't know it for certain, she felt it, as if complete and utter happiness was lying just beyond her reach.

But would she grab it and hold on? Or would she allow it to slip between her fingers? She didn't want to fall in love, to turn her life over to an emotion she couldn't control. It was far more sensible to distance herself from this man. Though her mind told her one thing, Marisol's heart contradicted every fear.

She wrapped her arms around his neck and Ian buried his face between her breasts, the two of them now caught in the vortex of their desire. As her need began to build and her release grew closer, Marisol allowed both her body and her mind to surrender to him.

Her orgasm came upon her slowly this time, a single shudder and then another. He buried himself even deeper inside her and then moaned and it was only then that she felt the explosion of sensation. Who was this man who made her feel so powerful, yet so completely defenseless?

She nuzzled his soft hair, weaving her fingers through it and arching against him one last time. She couldn't let herself love him, but Marisol was left to wonder if she already did.

DECLAN DROPPED the file folder in the center of Ian's desk, then took a seat in one of the office chairs. "It's all there," he said. "Marisol Arantes and David Barnett."

"When I called, I thought I told you I didn't want you to do a check on her. Just on him."

Declan shrugged. "Well, I did it anyway." He pointed to the folder. "Go ahead. Read it. I think you'll be interested in what we found."

Ian pushed the folder back across the desk to his brother. "Nah. I don't need to know anything about her."

"You're a cop, aren't you?" Declan replied, watching him shrewdly.

Ian glanced up at his brother. "Why? Is she in trouble?"

"Not *in* trouble," Dec said. "More like, she *is* trouble." He paused. "What is this woman to you?"

"I don't know," Ian said. "I'm just curious. She's been causing some problems in town. And I caught Barnett breaking into her gallery a few nights ago. She said they used to be engaged, but I think something's going on there."

"I'd say more than something," Dec replied.

"What?"

His brother stood and nodded at the folder. "Just read it. I think you'll find that Marisol Arantes is connected to some pretty shady characters, the kind of characters that the police chief of Bonnett Harbor might take a particular interest in."

With that, Dec turned and walked out of Ian's office, leaving the folder sitting on the desk. Ian reached out and ran his hand over it, tracing the logo of Dec's company with his fingertip. Did he really want to know what was inside? Or was it better to just let it go?

This was his fault. He could have insisted that they

learn more about each other, that they at least spend a day or two discussing their pasts. But it seemed that the moment he saw Marisol, all he could think about was sex. If he spent as much time getting to know her as he did trying to seduce her, he could probably write her biography.

But did he really care about the silly details of her past? What counted was the time they spent together in the present. And in the present, she was the perfect woman for him—no matter what Declan thought.

Ian grabbed the folder and shoved it into the top drawer of his desk, then strode out of the office. But halfway down the hall, he turned around and went back to retrieve it. If he was going to allow himself to need this woman, then he deserved to know everything about her—the good and bad. And if the bad was very bad, then he'd be better off knowing.

With the folder tucked under his arm, Ian walked to the front desk and grabbed a radio, then told Sally to call him if he was needed. He decided to walk the seven blocks to Gallerie Luna, hoping the exercise would help him decide what to do.

But by the time he reached Bay Street, the answer was no clearer. Though his curiosity was killing him, he was afraid to learn something that might ruin his relationship with Marisol.

The front door to the gallery was propped open and Ian peeked inside. He saw Marisol standing over a huge canvas that she'd laid flat on the floor. Her hands were hitched on her waist and her hair tumbled around her face as she stared down at the painting in progress. She wore a baggy T-shirt and a pair of pants that ended just below the knee, showing off the pretty curve of her calf.

He watched her for a long time as she dabbed paint onto the canvas, then stepped back to look at her work. He was tempted to turn around and walk away, and to dump the file in the nearest trash bin. But instead, he stepped inside.

She heard his approach and turned. A smile broke across her face and she dropped her brush in a nearby coffee can and ran across the room. Throwing her arms around his neck, she kissed him. Ian held her body against his and thought about how easy it was to take her into his arms. There was no longer any clumsiness or hesitation. It was as if they'd been together for ages and just knew how they fit, her hips against his, his hands spanning her tiny waist, her fingers furrowed through the hair at his nape.

"I was hoping you'd stop by," she said. Marisol grabbed his hand and pulled him along behind her. "You have to see. I've been working on this all day and it's just happening. I don't even have to think, I just paint."

The painting was of a nude in a familiar pose. "That's me?"

She nodded. "It's not finished. But I can already tell it's going to be perfect. See across the shoulders, how there's a sense of movement. As if I've caught you shifting beneath the light. It's powerful and alive."

Ian could see what she meant and he was surprised

at how her simple charcoal sketches had been transformed into a painting.

"You have to pose for me again tonight. There's something else I want to try." She clasped her hands in front of her. "This could be a series. I don't usually paint on a canvas this large, but I think it works. It just has to be big, don't you agree?" She took a deep breath, then sighed. "I could use something to eat. Why don't we go out and celebrate?"

Ian scrambled for an excuse. He and Marisol had kept their affair quiet for this long for no particular reason. He was ready to pay up on the bet with his brothers any time they might ask. But Bonnett Harbor was a small town and rumors usually began small and escalated. The police chief involved with the town's newest resident would provide plenty of titillating gossip, especially if there was sex involved. And Marisol's art made her the subject of plenty of speculation.

But now there was something else to add to the mix. If Marisol was involved in something shady, then he couldn't afford to make his relationship with her public. The last thing he needed was a scandal to drag him down. "I'd love to," Ian said, "but I'm still on the clock."

"You don't even have time for dinner?"

"It's two in the afternoon," he said. "It's lunchtime, not dinnertime."

Marisol giggled. "All right, lunch then."

Ian shook his head. "Sorry."

"Dinner later?"

"I have to work this evening," he lied. "Why don't I call you?"

She gave him a confused look, then shrugged. "All right. But can you at least stay for a snack? I've got some ice-cream sandwiches in the fridge."

He nodded and Marisol hurried off to the small kitchen in the back of the gallery. When she returned, she pulled him over to the sofa and sat down on one end. "So, if things continue to go well, I think I should open the gallery in three weeks. That means I have to get invitations printed up and hire a caterer and figure out what to do about parking." She took a bite of the ice-cream sandwich, then handed it to him. "You're going to be famous, you know."

"Why?"

"And you have to be at the opening. Everyone will want to see my muse." She reached out and ran a finger down his forearm, sending him a tantalizing smile. "Unless you want to be my secret muse?"

"Maybe that would be best," Ian said. "I'd prefer that my ass stay incognito in this town."

"You're my secret lover, too," Marisol said. "Does that make it more exciting for you?"

"Maybe," he replied. "Have you told anyone about us?"

"I'm not sure what I'd say," she replied. "I'm not sure what's going on with us. I know we're lovers and…"

Ian nodded. "And?"

She pushed up on her knees and crawled over to him, then wrapped her arms around his neck and gave him a lingering kiss. When she drew back, her gaze met his and for a long moment, Marisol searched his face.

She kissed him again and he tried to react normally, but it was as if she were testing him, evaluating his response. The conversation had suddenly turned serious. When she looked at him again, it was there in her eyes—a tiny hint of sadness and resignation, bewilderment and then acceptance.

Marisol forced a smile. "You know, I should really get back to work," she said, her tone cool and indifferent. "And I'm sure you have speeding tickets to write and criminals to arrest."

She jumped off the couch and wandered back over to her painting, turning her attention to the canvas. Ian stood, not quite sure how he ought to leave things. He'd almost forgotten their time together would probably end, and sooner rather than later. He'd been so caught up in the excitement, in biding the hours until the next moment he'd be able to touch her or kiss her, that he hadn't planned for this or even run it over in his head. But this was reality, not the fantasy life that they'd been living.

Was this it? Was this the beginning of the end for them? In the past, there had always been accusations and anger, a long list of his faults and explanations of how it should have been. With Marisol, it wouldn't be so dramatic. She'd simply let go of his hand and walk away, no regrets and no doubts.

Perhaps their relationship was just a sexual flash fire, burning hot and bright for a short time before quickly smothering itself. He didn't want to walk away and it took every ounce of his willpower to move to the door. "I'll call you," he said.

"Or I'll call you," she replied, not even looking at him.

He nodded, the unread file still clutched in his hand. He didn't bother to glance back, knowing that he'd only question his choice to leave. Ian didn't need to be reminded of how beautiful Marisol was, or how her smile had the capacity to make him feel as if he owned the world. Or how being with her had become his primary reason for getting up in the morning.

Ian opened the door and stepped out into the bright afternoon light. A little more than a week ago, he'd been content with his life, happy with his work and hopeful that his social life might improve. And then he'd spent the most incredible week caught up in an affair with a sexy stranger. In the end, what had he really lost?

As he strolled down the sidewalk, Ian decided the best course of action would be to shred the file the moment he got back to the station. It didn't matter what Declan had found. Until Marisol Arantes did something illegal on his watch, in his jurisdiction, she was just another citizen of Bonnett Harbor.

And what he didn't know wouldn't hurt him.

6

MARISOL PACED back and forth across the length of the gallery, counting each step in an attempt to distract her mind. It was nearly midnight and she hadn't slept more than a few hours in the past two days. She'd been operating on caffeine and confusion, her mind filled with thoughts of Ian Quinn.

Over and over again, she'd tried to explain to herself how things had gone from so good to so bad in the blink of an eye. The moment he'd walked into the gallery Tuesday afternoon, she'd known something was wrong. He couldn't seem to look at her for more than a few seconds, and the moment she'd kissed him, she'd felt him pull away.

The end hadn't come as a surprise. But the way it had ended still didn't make sense. She was missing a piece of the puzzle, some clue to his behavior that could help make it all become clear. At first, she suspected that he might have found out about her father. But why wouldn't he have simply confronted her and asked her about Hector Arantes? He certainly couldn't know about the painting. She'd kept it well hidden and David had left town the night Ian had almost arrested him.

Had he grown bored? She stopped her pacing and closed her eyes, trying to remember that night in the gallery, when she had sketched him. Their passion had been mutual, there was no question about that. So how had it cooled so quickly?

Marisol wasn't one to sit around and guess at the answers to her questions. Grabbing her keys, she headed to the door. A phone call first would only give him an excuse to brush her off. She'd go to Ian's house, and if he wasn't home, she'd wait for him.

The street outside the gallery was quiet, the heat of the day still radiating from the sidewalks. The sound of music drifted on the warm night air, entertainment from one of the nearby bars. Most of the citizens of Bonnett Harbor had turned in, but a few tourists still strolled the streets, looking for something to do on a Friday night.

Confronting Ian would be difficult, but they'd always been honest with each other. They could be that way now. Once she reached the street, Marisol stopped, a tiny sliver of doubt ruining her resolve. This shouldn't make a difference! He'd been nothing more than a brief infatuation. Or had he?

Marisol cursed to herself, then continued down the sidewalk to her car. She hadn't really paid attention to where Ian lived in Bonnett Harbor, but the town wasn't that big. And maybe driving around for a while would calm her nerves and wash away the frustration she felt.

In the end, she found Ian's house on the very first try, the Mustang parked in the driveway a clue that he was indeed home. She parked her car down the block, then walked beneath the huge maples that lined both sides of the street, the night breeze rustling the leaves overhead.

When she reached his house, she stood at the front door for a long time, unable to make herself ring the bell. What was she doing? Was she that desperate to have him that she couldn't stay away?

She reached for the bell and, at the last moment, tried the door. To her surprise, it was unlocked. She pushed it open and stepped inside. The interior of the house was dark, illuminated only by the light that filtered through the windows from the street. Marisol waited for her eyes to adjust, then slowly wandered through the living room to the kitchen.

The surroundings were familiar, even in the dark, and she walked to the stairs and slowly climbed to the second floor. His bedroom was at the end of the hall and the door was open. The floor creaked and Marisol stopped, holding her breath and listening to the silence around her. A few seconds later, she continued until she reached his bed. She glanced around the room, not really sure what to do now that she was here.

Kneeling down beside the bed, she rested her arms on the mattress and studied his face. His hair fell in boyish waves across his forehead and he looked so much younger when he was asleep. Her fingers twitched and she fought the impulse to touch him, not sure if she planned to stay.

She reached out and skimmed her fingertip above his lip, his breath warm against her hand. And then, leaning over him, she kissed his mouth, so softly that he wouldn't awaken. But to her surprise, he opened his eyes.

They stared at each other for a long moment, then he jerked, pushing himself up on his elbows. Marisol sat back on her heels, her gaze still fixed on his face. She waited for him to speak, unwilling to make explanations for her presence.

When he didn't, she stood and reached for the buttons of her loose cotton dress. One by one, Marisol undid them until the dress gaped open. Then, she shrugged her shoulders and it fell to the floor around her feet, leaving her naked.

She didn't wait for an invitation, but as she stepped forward, he moved across the bed, lifting the sheet as he did. He was naked beneath and Marisol slipped in beside him. A heartbeat later, she was in his arms again. His lips came down on hers and he kissed her hungrily, roughly, the taste of his tongue warm and sweet in her mouth, the stubble of his beard sharp on her chin.

All her fears and doubts instantly dissipated as he ran his palms over her body. Ian touched every inch of her, as if he were reassuring himself that she was real and not just some vivid dream. And when he was satisfied, he began a lazy exploration, this time taking more care with each caress.

She sighed softly as his hands cupped her buttocks and pulled her hips against his. He was already hard and his erection pressed against her belly, branding her skin. He continued to kiss her, communicating his need without words, as if speaking might somehow break the spell that enveloped them both.

Marisol wasn't thinking about everything that had

gone wrong. Her thoughts were focused on everything that was right between them, a desire so deep that neither one them knew its limits.

His lips trailed along her jaw and then dropped to her shoulder, kisses mixed with a soft bite here and there. There was pleasure in the tiny bits of pain and it only seemed to make her need more urgent.

When he found her breast, she arched against him and he took her nipple into his mouth and sucked gently until it grew hard and sensitive. With every touch, every kiss, she surrendered a bit more of herself to him, and by the time he reached the spot between her legs, Marisol no longer had ownership of her responses.

When his tongue flicked at her clitoris, Marisol's breath caught in her throat. Every nerve in her body jolted, as if an electric shock had just shot through her. Every shred of her being focused on that one spot, on the delicious caress of his tongue and on the wild sensations that coursed through her.

She shifted until she could give him the same pleasure, taking his shaft into her mouth and then drawing back. Suddenly, every action was met by an equal reaction, and she wasn't sure whether she was initiating or receiving. It didn't really matter. They were caught in an endless circle of pleasure that came closer and closer to spinning out of control.

Marisol danced at the edge and she knew if she just let go, the pleasure would wash over her in waves. But she wanted more than what his tongue could give her.

Reaching down, she tangled her fingers in his hair and drew him away.

As if he sensed what she needed, he pulled her up to her knees and then wrapped his arms around her body from behind. His palms cupped her breasts and she reached back and grabbed his hips, pulling him tightly against her.

They tumbled forward, Marisol falling to her hands and knees. Ian grabbed her waist and slowly pushed inside her, burying himself deep. A low moan slipped from her throat, enough to tell him that she wanted more.

From that moment on, Marisol lost all sense of what was real. Every thought focused on the feel of his shaft, moving in and out of her. Each stroke brought her closer and closer to completion. And when he felt the shift in her desire, Ian increased his pace, driving harder and harder.

She couldn't touch him, couldn't see his face, but that didn't matter. The connection between them was relentlessly carnal, driving them both forward.

When her orgasm hit, she was unprepared for the power of it. No longer able to control herself, she fell forward and he went with her, shuddering as he found his release, as well.

They lay perfectly still except for the short gulps of breath they both required. Ian nuzzled his face into her hair and she listened as his breathing returned to normal. He slowly slipped out of her and when he was completely apart, he gathered her in his embrace and tucked her body against his.

They didn't speak. In truth, Marisol was afraid

to—afraid they'd go back to the strange, stilted conversation of the last time they were together. Maybe they weren't good at relationships. But they were fabulous at the sex.

Someday, that might not be enough. Someday, she might want something more. But for now, Ian's body was what she needed, his passion, his strength and his complete surrender.

IAN SAT QUIETLY in the dark, sprawled in an overstuffed chair near the bed. He'd been watching Marisol sleep for hours, listening to the soft rhythm of her breathing, noting the tiny movements of her fingers. He knew so many little things about her, things that might go unnoticed in a normal relationship, yet he seemed to find them particularly fascinating. Gradually, pieces were becoming a whole, but there were still huge gaps to fill, questions that needed to be answered.

When he'd first realized she was there beside his bed, he'd thought he was caught in a dream. But the moment she touched him, her warm, naked body against his skin, Ian knew she wasn't just a nighttime fantasy.

Over the past few days and nights, he'd done his best to put her out of his head. But it was clear by his reaction to her tonight that what he'd thought was progress had simply been a feeble attempt at denial. His body still responded to hers. If anything, he wanted her more for having been without her for three days.

Finding pleasure in her was his body's ultimate betrayal. But it wasn't just the physical act of coming inside of her that he craved. His orgasm had become more about possession than release. Every moment he spent in such intimate contact was a moment that bound her to him.

Marisol was his. Her body, her soul, her heart, her mind, he wanted them all. He couldn't imagine relinquishing her to another man, knowing what they'd shared. But how far would he go to keep her in his life?

She stirred and Ian leaned forward, bracing his arms on his knees. At first, he thought she'd go back to sleep, but then Marisol pushed up on her elbow and searched the bed for him, reaching out to touch his pillow.

"I'm here," he murmured.

She turned, brushing the hair out of her eyes. "Is it morning?"

He shook his head. "No. Go back to sleep."

She snuggled down beneath the covers and sighed. "Your front door was unlocked. You shouldn't leave your front door unlocked."

"My brother Declan stays here occasionally when he's in town. Sometimes he forgets his key. Besides, who's going to break into my house? I'm the police chief."

"I broke in," she said with a self-satisfied smile.

"But you didn't come to steal anything." He paused. "On second thought, maybe you did." She'd stolen his willpower, his resolve and his self-control. And yet somehow, she didn't make him feel weak or inadequate. And he certainly wasn't a victim.

Being with Marisol made him more alive than he'd ever been. Losing himself in her body, in their lovemaking, made him realize what it was to be a man. He reveled in their differences, in the perfect contrasts between their bodies, soft and hard, delicate and strong, woman and man.

He and Marisol had been fashioned by fate to be together. It was the only explanation for the sheer exhilaration he felt when he touched her, and the contentment that seemed to descend upon them both when they were finished.

"Are you sorry I came?" she asked.

He shook his head. "How could I be?"

"I couldn't sleep," she said. "I just needed to sleep. I needed you."

Ian nodded. "Sometimes, I feel as if we've known each other for years. And then, I realize I don't know anything about you, beyond the fact that we share this incredibly intimate relationship. I can possess your body in any way I choose and you wouldn't refuse me, would you?"

She shook her head.

"But yet, I could ask you a simple question, and suddenly, a wall would spring up between us."

"That would depend on the question," she said. "Is there a question you've been wanting to ask me?"

"Yeah," Ian said. "But I don't know what use it would be asking since I don't think you're willing to answer."

"Then don't ask," she said, her voice taking on an uneasy tone.

"I have to, Marisol. If I don't, then I'm going against everything I am."

She sat up in bed and pulled the covers around her breasts, her eyes wide and watching. Ian thought again about how best to handle her. He'd always been an honest man, yet suddenly, he'd begun living in this world of unspoken lies and half truths, content that if he didn't acknowledge the problem then it didn't exist.

"A few days ago, my brother Declan gave me some information…about you. And about David Barnett."

She raked her hair out of her eyes, a frown wrinkling her brow. "I don't—what kind of information?"

Ian sat back in the chair, stretching his legs out in front of him and tipping his head back to stare at the ceiling. He couldn't look at her. Her beauty just blinded him to reality. All he could do was listen to her voice and gauge her reactions that way. "He did a background check on you both."

"Just like that? How did he know to—"

"I asked him to do it. The night after I met David Barnett." So it was half a lie, but right now, Ian couldn't feel guilty. She was hiding something from him—every instinct told him so. "I just got a vibe off of him that he might be trouble." He looked at Marisol. "I'm a cop and I have been for a long time. I can't ignore those hunches. It's part of the job."

"So why check up on me?"

"Even though we'd been…intimate, I didn't know anything about you. Call it self-preservation."

"And what did you learn?"

"You tell me," he said, anger edging his voice.

She caught her bottom lip between her teeth and

stared at her hands, her fingers plucking at the sheet twisted around her legs. "I can't," she whispered.

"You can't? Or you won't?" He cursed softly. "Tell me you can't because there was nothing in that file. Tell me all these doubts racing through my head don't exist. Tell me I *do* know the woman I've been sleeping with. Because if you don't, them I'm going to feel like a real chump."

Silence spun out around them and Ian expected any moment she'd crawl out of bed, grab her dress and leave. "Marisol, you know you can trust me," he whispered.

"Can I? How do I know that? We met, what? Ten days ago? Just because a lot has happened in those ten days, doesn't mean I can trust you. I thought I could trust David Barnett and I was wrong."

"So you would rather I just let this go? Just walk away from you and all of this, from whatever is in that folder?"

Marisol nodded. "You can't help me," she murmured. "It would put everything you stand for at risk. You're a police officer and you're not allowed to bend the rules." She paused. "Why don't you just tell me what you know and I'll tell you if it's true?"

"I threw the file away," Ian said. "I didn't look inside. I don't know what you're hiding. That's up to you to say. But if it's something that will get you in trouble with the law, then you know what has to happen."

"You have to stay away from me," she said.

Ian cursed. They were caught in a trap, only one of them able to break free, but at the expense of the other. Deep down, he knew she was in trouble and she was probably mixed up in something illegal. But the moment he learned the facts, he'd be compelled to act in his capacity as an officer of the law. He also sensed that she needed his help, but she couldn't ask for fear that she'd draw him into the mess.

"I haven't done anything wrong," she said, after a long silence. "You have to believe me. I'm just trying to protect someone I love."

"Then you love him?"

"Of course I do," she said.

Ian's jaw grew tense and he bit back a curse. So that was how it was. She was still in love with David Barnett and probably sleeping with him now, too. It couldn't be any clearer than that. "Maybe this is for the best," he said. The words came out of his mouth, but Ian didn't believe them for a second. "You take care of your business and I'll handle mine and we'll go on as if we never met."

"But we did meet," she said.

He nodded. "As long as you keep yourself out of trouble, I'll leave you alone. If you cause any problems, Marisol, you're not going to give me a choice."

"I understand," she said.

Ian levered to his feet then circled the bed and picked up her dress from the floor. He held it out to her. "You'd better get dressed. I'll take you home."

Marisol took the dress from him and slipped it over her head, then fumbled with the buttons. When she was finished, she crawled out of bed and searched the floor for her shoes. "I have my car. I'll go."

When she was ready, Marisol stood in front of him

and touched his face with her hand. "I know what I'm doing," she murmured. "You have to trust me on this." She pushed up on her toes and pressed a kiss to his lips. "I would never hurt you."

With that, she turned and walked out. Ian stood alone, wondering at how the room had suddenly turned cold. He felt as if everything he'd ever wanted had been snatched from him and there was nothing he could do about it. Marisol wasn't his, she never had been. He'd just been too caught up in the fantasy to realize that.

"WHAT ARE YOU GOING TO DO?"

Marisol sat on the edge of her worktable, her legs dangling. She had thought about that question since the moment she'd unwrapped the painting and realized what her father had done. And she would have come to a decision a lot sooner if Ian hadn't been occupying her thoughts day and night.

It wasn't any wonder she preferred to think about him. The sexy man who made her writhe with pleasure, or a potential problem that could get her thrown in jail? The choice wasn't difficult. In truth, she'd been using Ian to distract herself from her problems, to avoid the inevitable choice that she'd have to make.

Marisol looked up at Sascha and forced a smile. Her friend had arrived early that morning. They'd spent most of the day going over the pieces Sascha wanted for her own gallery, and the work Marisol would show at her opening. They discussed the prices they'd attach to each painting and sculpture.

All day long, Marisol had waited for the right moment to broach the subject of her plan, praying that Sascha would agree to help her. The waning afternoon had finally pushed her into action, Marisol knowing that Sascha would have to leave soon in order to get back to the city before dark. "I came up with an idea. But I'm going to need your help."

"My help?"

"Don't worry. I'm not going to ask you to do anything illegal."

Sascha shifted nervously. "I think helping you replace that painting would probably make me an accessory to some sort of crime. I adore accessories, but I don't want to be one, darling."

"We're not going to get caught." Though Marisol's words sounded convincing, her confidence didn't extend much further.

"All right, what's the plan?"

She jumped off the table and took Sascha's hand, dragging her to the far wall of the gallery. "See this," she said, pointing to the painting she'd been working on all night. "This is a gift. I'm going to present it to the Templetons. It just happens to be exactly the same size as their Colter."

Sascha peered at the painting, her smile slowly growing. "Oh, I saw this in a movie! The real painting is underneath and then you'll spray it with—"

"No!" Marisol said. "Nothing that complicated.

I'll crate this with the Colter and get them both into the Templetons' house. Then I'll make a fuss about unveiling my gift in the library, where the Colter is hung. And then, you'll create a diversion and I'll switch the two."

"A diversion?"

Marisol ran over to her worktable and returned with the handheld hot air gun she used to dry paint. "You'll excuse yourself and go to the powder room under the stairs. Then you'll plug this in, fill the sink with water and toss it into the sink. Or, I suppose you could use the toilet. Either way, the power should go off which will give me enough time to switch the paintings."

"Most of those security systems have a battery backup," Sascha warned.

"I know. But if the alarm sounds, the Templetons will think it's from the power surge. Even if they suspect something is going on, they have far more valuable pieces in other parts of the house. The Renoir in the foyer is worth five times as much as the Colter. And rumor has it they have a Picasso drawing upstairs in the master suite."

Sascha picked up the dryer. "How am I supposed to get this into the house?"

Marisol rolled her eyes. "Come on. You don't have a designer bag that could carry that?"

"I suppose I could carry my Balenciaga. Although, I haven't found anything good to wear with it yet. We'll have to go shopping."

"I don't care if you stuff the thing under your shirt,"

Marisol said. "It's your responsibility to get it into the house and make sure the electricity is off for at least five minutes. I'll take care of the rest."

"But there are so many things that could go wrong," Sascha said. "And what if they do?"

"Then I'll tell the Templetons the truth and throw myself on their mercy. But I have to at least give this a try first. My motives are honorable. I'm attempting to right a wrong, so this isn't really a crime, is it?"

"Well, when you put it that way, I guess it isn't. Although I'm not sure your little friend, Officer Studly, would agree."

Marisol winced. "I want you to call the Templetons and tell them I have a gift for them. You set up the get-together and I'll make sure the plan works."

"Speaking of Officer Studly, where does he fit into this plan?"

"He doesn't," Marisol said. "He doesn't know anything about it."

That wasn't entirely true, she mused. Ian knew something was going on, he just wasn't sure what. Since he was leaving it up to her to tell him, then he'd just have to wait until it was all over and her father was safe.

"Are you still sleeping with him?"

Marisol considered her answer for a long moment. She'd slept with him last night but had no intentions of sleeping with him tonight, so technically she wasn't *still* sleeping with him. Ian had made himself perfectly clear. Until she told him the truth about herself, he wasn't interested in associating with her.

Still, Marisol had to wonder if he'd invite her back into his bed if she made the offer. Would he be able to turn her away? Or was his desire for her more powerful than his professional ethics?

Every night they spent together seemed to bring them closer and closer. Last night, after she'd crawled into her own bed, she'd lain awake for hours, trying to figure out a way to tell him the truth, a way to ask for his help, if only so they might be together again.

She knew him sexually, knew every inch of his body, knew exactly how he'd respond to her touch. Yet she could only guess at how he'd react to her revelation. She knew the man who made love to her with such reckless abandon, but she didn't know the man who put on a uniform and spent his days enforcing the law.

Marisol wanted to know that man, but at the same time, he held such power over her—the power to take her father away from her again. No, she couldn't trust him. Not now, not yet. Sascha was the only person who knew the truth and it would have to stay that way until she sorted out this mess.

"Well, are you going to answer my question?" Sascha asked.

"Am I still sleeping with him?"

"That's what I asked. Either you are or you aren't."

"No. In fact, he knows something's going on with me…and David. He has—he had a file on us both."

"What?"

Marisol held out her hand to calm Sascha's rising

panic. "It's all right. He didn't read it, but he has suspicions about me."

"What kind of cop is he?"

"I think he might be afraid of what he'll learn," Marisol admitted.

Sascha gasped. "He's in love with you."

"Don't be silly," Marisol cried.

"I'm not. He's a cop who suspects you might be involved in criminal activity and yet he's unwilling to even figure out what you're up to. He's in love with you."

"We barely know each other." Marisol turned away from Sascha and began to arrange her tubes of paint on the wide surface of the worktable. Was Sascha right? After all, why wouldn't Ian appease his natural curiosity by reading the file on her? She drew a deep breath and tried to sort it all out in her mind. Was it because he didn't care? Or because he cared too much?

"I have to find a place to hide the painting," Marisol murmured. "David showed up a few nights ago and I think he was trying to break in here and steal it back. If he gets it, there's no way I can fix this for my father."

"Where can you put it?"

"You could take it," she suggested. "Hide it at your place until we're ready to make the switch."

Sascha shook her head. "Not a chance. I agreed to help you with your little plan, but that extends to creating a diversion. If I get caught with that painting, my career would be over."

"I understand."

Marisol considered all her options and could think of

only one other place that it would be perfectly safe. She smiled to herself. "There is one place that David would never think to look."

7

IAN STARED AT HIS CARDS, then shrewdly searched for tells on the faces of Declan and Marcus. "I'll call," he finally said, tossing in three blue poker chips. He laid down his cards. "Kings over sixes."

Declan cursed and threw his cards into the center of the table. "I can't buy a decent hand," he muttered. Shoving his chair back, he stood. "Does anyone want another beer?"

"I'm good," Marcus said.

"Me, too," Ian murmured.

Declan wandered over to the small kitchen on the far wall of Marcus's loft and opened the refrigerator. When he returned, he carried a fresh beer and a bag of potato chips. He sprawled into the chair, groaning softly. "I guess I'm sleeping on your sofa tonight," he said, tipping his beer bottle toward Marcus. "I'm too drunk to drive back to Providence. Or I could stay with you." He pointed his beer at Ian and grinned. "I prefer that nice soft bed in your guest room to Marky's sofa."

Ian shook his head. "I have an early day tomorrow. Besides, I walked over and I'm not about to drag you home through the streets of Bonnett Harbor stumbling drunk."

It was a logical excuse considering Ian didn't want any houseguests. After Marisol's surprise appearance in his bedroom the night before last, he half expected her to turn up again. And he didn't need his brother questioning the strange frantic moans coming from Ian's room in the middle of the night. Or the beautiful woman sneaking out the kitchen door in the hours before dawn. He'd managed to keep his affair with Marisol completely private, no small feat for a public figure in Bonnett Harbor. He wasn't about to let that change.

"You can sack out here," Marcus offered. "Since I'm the only one still sober enough to drive, I'll head back over to Newport and sleep on the boat." He gathered up his poker chips and cashed them in, then stuffed the money into his jeans pocket. "Can I drop you at your place?" he asked Ian.

"If you're dropping him off, you can drop me off," Dec asked.

"I'm going to walk," Ian insisted. "The fresh air will clear my head." He took a small share of the pot for himself, then pushed the remainder across the table at Declan.

His brother cursed as he counted out the money in front of him. "I can't figure how you tossers always win."

Marcus rolled his eyes as he looked over at Ian. Once Declan had a few beers in him, he was an encyclopedia of tells, every emotion written on his face. Both of them had always known it, but they weren't about to reveal their secrets. "Just luck," Ian murmured.

"I can't wait to collect on our other bet," Declan said. "I think Ian is already wavering. What do you say, Marky? Is Ian going to be the first to fall to his lustful urges?"

Marcus's eyebrow shot up. "Ian has never been one to deny himself anything."

And Marcus had always had the knack for cutting right to the point. Ian had come to the conclusion that he had no self-control when it came to Marisol. Every promise he'd ever made to himself to step back, to temper his desire, to fight his attraction, had been broken. And after their last encounter, Ian couldn't ignore his feelings for her any longer. He was obsessed, an addict whose only vice in life was Marisol's body. He couldn't imagine a time in the near or distant future when he wouldn't want her.

"A pact is a pact," Ian said. "We swore on our lucky charm."

Marcus held up his key chain, the little gold medallion dangling from it.

"That's right," Dec said emphatically, slamming his beer bottle down on the table. "And since you two blokes are so weak and pathetic when it comes to women, I give you permission to sleep with as many as you want. I plan to prove there isn't a woman out there who can tempt me."

"There isn't a woman out there who wants to tempt you," Marcus muttered.

Dec pointed his beer bottle at Marcus, sending him a menacing glare. "You can shut your mouth anytime, little brother."

"And you can sleep on the street, big brother."

Declan laughed, holding up his hands in mock surrender. "All right. I won't make any more disparaging remarks. Anyone who lasts three months deserves the money. And since I know the only person who will last is me, then I deserve the money."

Marcus turned for the door. "I'll see you guys next weekend."

"Friday," Declan said. "Ian's cooking. Steaks at his place."

Ian frowned. "Since when?"

"Since I have to be in Boston all day Saturday and since you guys don't want to drive all the way to Providence. And since we can't go out to the pubs anymore because there are too many women."

"Fine," Ian said. "My place. Friday. Burgers, not steaks."

Marcus and Ian walked out together, down the stairs into the workroom and then out the door that opened onto the boatyard. "Maybe we shouldn't have made that bet," Ian said.

Marcus chuckled as he pulled open the door to his pickup. "I'm stuck on that boat, all alone. I've got it won, no matter how confident Dec feels."

"Of the three of us, he's the playboy in the bunch," Ian commented. "All it will take is the right woman and he'll be off and running." Ian stepped away from the truck then waved as Marcus drove past him to the street.

The night was warm and still, small sounds magnified in the silence. A dog barked in the distance and he could hear the gentle hum of air conditioners as he passed by a row of shops. He didn't even realize he was on Bay Street until he stood in front of Gallerie Luna.

Ian stared at the front windows, thinking back to the sculptures that had first brought him here, to that first day he'd met Marisol. It had only been two weeks, yet his life had been completely changed.

Ian sighed and closed his eyes, raking his hand through his hair. He knew the sound of her voice and the taste of her mouth, the way her hands felt on his skin and the scent of her hair. He knew what made her laugh and what made her moan with pleasure. And just that was more than he'd ever known about a woman in the past.

How had so much changed in such a short time? Two weeks ago, he'd bet his brothers he could avoid women for three months. And almost immediately, he'd found himself caught up in a wildly satisfying sexual whirlwind, unable to control his desire—or perhaps unwilling.

There were times when he wished he could go back and do it all again, to stick to the plan and stay away from Marisol. Maybe then he might have been able to master his impulses. Still, it would have only been a matter of time before he found himself drawn into her orbit.

He walked to the front door of the gallery and peered inside, but the lights were off. Resisting the urge to ring the bell, Ian turned from the door and retreated back to the sidewalk.

For all intents and purposes, it was over between him and Marisol. He'd given her a choice, honesty or him, and she'd chosen to keep her secrets. The need would fade with each day that passed, and in a month or two, he'd be able to pass an hour or even a full day without thinking of her.

For now, Marisol Arantes was no more than a citizen of Bonnett Harbor. If she caused trouble, he would be forced to involve himself in her life again. But if she kept to herself and didn't break the law, then he had no excuse to see her.

Ian continued his walk home, his mind replaying images of Marisol, dressed and undressed, awake and asleep, aroused and sated, like an erotic movie in his head. Did he really believe he could do without her? He'd always achieved anything he set his mind to, so why was he suddenly doubting himself? She was a woman and women came and went in his life without much fanfare.

Cursing softly, he picked up his pace, his walk turning to a jog and then to a run. He ran until his chest burned and his breath came in ragged gasps. He ran until he reached his house, then ran around the block a few more times. When he was finally exhausted, Ian returned to his house, threw the back door open and stumbled inside.

The house was quiet and cool and Ian moved comfortably in the darkness. He grabbed a bottle of water from the refrigerator and cracked it open, then took a long drink. But his mind immediately returned to the last night they'd spent together, in his bed.

He wondered if she'd come again that night and a twinge of anticipation twisted at his gut. "Damn her," he muttered. Ian turned to walk to the front of the house, but froze when he saw a figure outlined in the doorway.

He closed his eyes and drew a deep breath, then opened them again. She was still there. Slowly, she walked toward him and Ian held his breath, waiting for her to simply evaporate before his eyes. But when she touched him, he knew she wasn't a mirage.

Marisol nuzzled his chest, gently pushing him back against the counter. The water bottle fell to the floor and Ian braced his hands behind him as she slowly worked at the buttons of his shirt. Her lips traced a path, lower and lower, with each button she opened. And when she reached the bottom, she undid the button on his jeans.

His gaze fixed on her, his head down, and in the corner of his mind, he knew he ought to resist. But her forbidden seduction teased at his imagination, making every sensation more intense. Her fingers grasped the waistband of his jeans and she pulled them down around his hips, along with his boxers. An instant later, her lips surrounded him, gently drawing his cock into her mouth.

Desire slammed through his body, feelings so powerful his head began to buzz. Ian tried to think, to put what was happening to him into perspective, to find a way to rationalize his surrender. But instinct had overwhelmed lucid thought and Ian gave himself over to the extraordinary damp and warmth of her lips and tongue.

She knew him so well, knew every little thing that spiked his desire and left him aching for more. It was so easy to want her, to know that every time they were together it would be perfectly satisfying. Would another woman ever know his body so well?

Ian sucked in a sharp breath as she ran her tongue along his shaft, from tip to base. Like delicious torture, she began to move faster, picking up her pace until he could no longer delay. Desperate to be closer, Ian reached down and pulled her to her feet.

His hands tore at her clothes, caressing each bit of skin that he revealed. It only took a few moments and she was naked, her body outlined by soft moonlight coming through the window above the sink. He quickly shed the rest of his clothes, then began a gentle exploration of her body, smoothing his hands over every curve, every tempting bit of flesh.

Marisol did the same, her fingers dancing lightly over his naked skin, teasing and caressing, continuing the seduction she'd begun with her mouth. Every time he was with Marisol, her body seemed to reveal something new and intriguing, a soft spot of skin he hadn't yet discovered, a place where his touch made her breath quicken and her need increase.

It became a tantalizing game, a battle to see who knew the other better, who would ultimately surrender to the perfect caress. How would he ever let her go? *Why* would he? Ian couldn't imagine ever tiring of her or ever wanting another woman more. Marisol was his and his alone.

He grabbed her waist and spun her around, then lifted her up to sit on the edge of the counter. Slowly, Ian spread her legs, then guided himself inside her. Inch by inch, she surrounded him with her heat, until he was buried to the hilt.

He captured her face with his hands and kissed her deeply, thirsting for the sweet taste of her mouth. No matter how close he was, how deep he was, it didn't seem to be enough anymore. There had to be more— words, whispers, proof that she felt the same as he did, that there was meaning behind what they shared.

"I can't breathe without wanting you," he murmured, biting at her lower lip. "What have you done to me, Marisol? How am I supposed to live without this?"

She wrapped her legs around his hips and Ian carried her into the living room. But when they reached the stairs, he realized he couldn't go on any longer, the shift of her body against him bringing him close to the edge. He gently laid her down on the stairs, then braced his hands on either side of her.

Slowly, he pulled out, the simple movement causing a flood of desire to course through his body. When he didn't slide back inside her, Marisol moaned, moving beneath him, her hands grasping at his hips.

"Say it," he whispered. "Tell me you want me."

She pulled against him, but he drew back. "I do," she breathed. "I do want you."

"Forever," he said. "Tell me it will be forever." He needed to hear the words, even though they might not be true. He had to believe, somewhere, in some corner of her heart, she felt the same connection he did.

Her eyes stared up at him, clear and sober. "Forever," she repeated. "I will want you forever."

With that Ian plunged back inside, feverishly driving into her as she writhed against him. And when she finally cried out, her orgasm racking her body with pleasure, Ian pulled her hips tight against his and allowed himself to yield. Caught in the midst of a shattering orgasm, he felt as if he could almost touch heaven.

They slid down along the steps, their limbs tangled, bodies moist with perspiration. Ian smoothed the hair from her damp brow and took in the beauty of her face. There was no use denying it any longer. Maybe he'd known it all along. He was falling in love with Marisol Arantes. And even if he could stop himself, Ian didn't want to.

MARISOL SIGHED SOFTLY and sat up, brushing her hair out of her eyes. She glanced over at Ian, sleeping next to her, his face buried in the pillow, his arm curled around his head.

She reached out and smoothed a lock of his hair from his forehead. The lines of tension that usually creased his brow were gone and he seemed so much more relaxed than he had in the past week. It was her fault. She was making this more difficult than it need be. If she really cared about Ian's feelings, then she'd spend her nights in her own bed and stop tormenting him. But instead, Marisol chose to be selfish, to satisfy her own needs.

This was the only place she felt safe, in Ian's arms, in his bed. The rest of her life had become one big anxiety—her father, the gallery opening, her future as an artist—and that damned painting. If she wanted to worry, there was plenty to worry about. But when she was with Ian, all her troubles seemed to disappear, if only for a short time. The moment he touched her, her mind and body were swept away to another place.

She carefully crawled out of bed and searched for her clothes, then remembered they were downstairs in the kitchen.

"Stay."

Marisol turned and looked at Ian. He'd pushed up on his elbow and was watching her, his hair mussed, his eyes wide. "It's starting to get light," she said. "I should go."

"Don't. I want you to stay."

She smiled. "And what will the gossips say? Aren't you worried about your reputation?"

His jaw twitched, the movement barely visible in the pale morning light.

"Whenever we talk lately, it seems to end in an argument," Marisol said. "Perhaps it's just better to be silent."

"How can that be better?" Ian asked.

"Not better, just more sensible."

"I like to hear the sound of your voice," he said. "It doesn't matter what you say. Just talk to me, Marisol."

"About what?"

"Anything. I'm beginning to think that I dream you into my bed, that you're not really here. When I wake up you're gone and all I'm left with is the smell of your hair on my pillow." He reached out and grabbed her hand, then pulled her back onto the bed. "Tell me a story. I don't care what it's about, I just need to hear your voice." He pulled her naked body against his, throwing his leg over her hip and kissing her softly. "Tell me about your childhood."

She closed her eyes for a long moment, relaxing into his arms again and letting her thoughts drift. "There aren't a lot of things I remember, but I do remember the first time I picked up a paintbrush."

"Tell me," he whispered as he kissed the skin below her ear.

"My mother insists I was only three, but the memory is so vivid I think I must have been older." Marisol snuggled against him. "We were still living in Portugal in a small town on the sea, not far from Lisbon. My father was painting and having modest success. My mother had just retired from dancing with a ballet company in Spain. And I was the center of their universe."

Ian pressed a kiss to the top of her head and Marisol smiled. She liked this feeling, this comfortable closeness. When they were like this, she could almost believe what they shared might last. "I'd sneaked into my father's studio while he was eating his lunch and all of his paints were there, such pretty colors in little tubes. So I grabbed a paintbrush and squeezed some of the paints out on the floor and began to apply them…to my body and to my clothes."

"You painted yourself?"

Marisol nodded, giggling at the memory. "I have photos of my very first work of art. My mother was horrified, but my father refused to let her clean me up. He felt that to do so would have been stifling my creativity. And so I walked around our little village for days, covered in colorful paint, like a pretty tropical bird. And the tourists took pictures of me and the old ladies fussed over me and my papa was so proud. I think that was the moment I decided I wanted to be an artist."

"I'd like to see the photos," Ian said. "Will you show me sometime?"

Marisol hesitated. They'd been so careful to maintain a distance between them, to avoid any talk of the future. Their relationship was supposed to be casual, no strings, no expectations. But now, Ian was changing the rules. He wanted to know who she was and where she'd come from. And "sometime" was the future, a date hovering off in the distance that required a promise of something more…forever.

Had he taken her words seriously? Had she made him a promise beyond the forever that was a night in his bed? Marisol knew she ought to beware, but at the same time, she needed to believe there was more to them than just this, a bed and two naked bodies.

"Now, you tell me a story," she said, attempting to shift focus back to him. "Tell me about your childhood."

"It wasn't nearly as perfect as yours," he said.

Marisol forced a smile. He didn't know about her father's trial and conviction, or about her mother's breakdown afterward, or the struggle that life had become for her. "When did you realize you wanted to become a policeman?"

"It wasn't such a clear choice for me," Ian said. "I spent most of my childhood wanting to be a rubbish man. A trash collector. They guy who stands on the back of the truck."

"Why?" Marisol asked.

"Survival," Ian replied. "My brothers and I were sent to Ireland when my ma got sick, and somehow we got it in our heads that we were going to run away and live on our own. Like *The Boxcar Children*."

"What are the boxcar children?"

"A book I read when I was young. About four orphan children who run away and live in an abandoned boxcar and find everything they need to live in a rubbish heap. Once my brother Declan and I realized that we weren't going home, we decided we'd run away. So we began to collect little items from the rubbish tips and hide them in the closet beneath the stairs at my grandmother's house."

"And did you run away?"

Ian shook his head. "My little brother, Marcus, talked us out of it. When we told him about our plans, he reminded us if we ran away and our parents came to fetch us, they wouldn't be able to find us. So it was better to stay put. It was only after I pulled my brothers out of a dozen school yard brawls that I decided law enforcement might be a good choice for me."

"It would have been an adventure to run away," she said.

"Our supplies got confiscated," Ian explained. "We started hiding food, fruit and bread and milk, and it started to smell really bad. My grandmother's cook found our stash and threw everything away."

"There were times when I was a kid I wanted to run away," she said. "My parents separated and my mother was…fragile. Needy. I raised myself and I'm not sure I did a very good job."

Ian tipped her chin up and gently kissed her. "I think you turned out real nice."

She giggled. "Thank you. And you turned out real nice, too."

"Another reason why we're perfect together," he teased.

"We are perfect together," she agreed. Marisol rolled over on top of him, stretching out until every inch of her naked skin was pressed against his. "See. We even fit perfectly."

Ian clasped her hands and stretched his arms out above his head. They lay together for a long time, her cheek resting on his shoulder, his breath warm on her temple. There were moments when her choices seemed so simple—Ian, passion; Ian, a future. But instead of focusing on those choices, she'd been forced to make her choices with her father in mind.

Would she have to suffer the consequences for his actions? Would his desperation destroy her chance for happiness? If there was a simple way out, she'd grab it. But it was too late to give the painting back to her father.

"Why didn't you read the file?" she asked. Marisol was afraid to look at him, afraid her question would open up another argument between them. "Didn't you want to know what was inside?"

"Maybe I should have," Ian said. "I guess I didn't want to ruin the illusion. I didn't want to trust what someone else had to say about you. I'd rather trust what I know."

"And what is that?"

"That you're beautiful and crazy and passionate. That you throw yourself into life like there's no tomorrow."

He paused. "Up until a few weeks ago, I was waiting around for my life to start, waiting for someone to appear and suddenly everything would make sense. But when I met you, I realized I'd have to go out and grab it and make it happen."

She untangled her fingers from his, then smoothed her palm over his cheek, kissing him, deeply and thoroughly. "You know I would tell you if I could," she murmured against his lips.

"I know you would tell me if you trusted me," he countered.

Marisol slowly drew away, smiling tremulously. "I should go."

"Promise you'll come back?"

She shrugged. "We'll see." She grabbed his robe and wrapped it around her naked body, then dropped one last kiss on his lips. "Go back to sleep."

Marisol walked out of the bedroom and down the stairs. She found her clothes where he had dropped them on the kitchen floor. As she dressed, she thought about returning to his bedroom. After all they'd shared, why couldn't she trust him? What was it that kept her from knocking down the last bricks in the wall she'd built around her heart?

It would be so easy to love Ian Quinn, like breathing, or smiling, no effort at all. Already, it felt as if he'd become a part of her life. She'd tried to sleep in her own bed, but it had become impossible. Having his arms around her, his naked body beside her, was stronger than any sleeping pill she could take.

Marisol tugged her dress over her head, then slipped her shoes onto her bare feet. "Don't," she murmured to herself, fighting the temptation to return to his bed. "Don't let yourself fall in love with him. Not now, not yet."

But as she walked into the quiet dawn, the sounds of the birds stirring in the trees, Marisol knew there wasn't much fight left in her. Ian Quinn had chipped away at her doubts and insecurities and she'd surrendered her body to him. How long would it be before he'd own her heart?

IAN STARED UP at the ceiling above his bed, looking at nothing but a gray expanse in the darkened bedroom. The soft sound of Marisol's breathing beside him did nothing to relax him. Sleep had eluded him once again and though his body was exhausted, his mind refused to go quiet.

Marisol lay naked next to him, her legs twisted in the sheets, her hair strewn about his pillow. For nearly a week, they'd been carrying on these midnight encounters, a physical relationship that was becoming more and more confusing with every day that passed.

What had begun a month ago as a normal little affair had turned into an intense, full-blown sexual obsession. For the past five nights, he'd indulged in nearly every fantasy he'd ever had, and some that he hadn't. Each night, he'd go to bed and wait for Marisol to appear. She'd sneak into his house, climb the stairs to his bedroom, slip out of her clothes and crawl into bed beside him. After that, they'd lose themselves in a long, slow seduction, two people bent on carnal pleasure.

And every night, it got a bit more desperate, as if they both knew the end was coming. Ian couldn't help but think they were simply avoiding the reality of their situation, both ignoring the lies that stood between them in favor of the passion that drew them together.

He'd reached the point where he was willing to have Marisol on her own terms, to enjoy what she offered without any thought to the future. They existed in some strange limbo, feeling emotions that would either gently die over time or burn them both up in white-hot flames. Ian couldn't see a pleasant end to it, no matter how he twisted it around and tried to make it work.

So, what choice did he have? To maintain his own ethical standards, he needed to know the truth. He'd perfected his interrogation techniques on the job in Providence. Maybe he ought to use them here. But he'd have to get Marisol out of her comfort zone, to shock her into realizing that she had no other choice but to confess what was written in the file that Declan had given him.

He crawled out of bed and wandered over to the window, pulling the curtains back to peer out onto the quiet street in front of his house. If only he could keep her here, it would give him time to convince her he could be trusted. But as with the past five nights, she'd wake before sunrise and slip out of bed, silently dressing then walking out without a word or even a farewell.

Ian glanced over at the bedside clock. It was nearly

4:00 a.m. and she'd be waking soon. If he wanted to keep her here, to broach the subject once again, he'd have to come up with a plan. Ian walked over to the closet and grabbed his utility belt from the hook on the door. He found his handcuffs in a small leather case on the belt and pulled them out.

She'd teased him about using the cuffs before. Why not take her up on her suggestion? He walked to the bed and gently took her wrist, snapping the cuff over it. But when he tried to attach the other bracelet to the bedpost, it wouldn't reach. In the end, he clipped it to his wrist, knowing she wouldn't be able to leave without his cooperation.

Lying beside her he closed his eyes and for the first time in days, he was able to relax, to retreat into a dreamless sleep, certain when he awoke, she would still be there.

Ian had barely slept, perhaps just a minute or two, when he was jolted awake by a sharp slap to his chest. He groaned softly and opened his eyes. The clock read four thirty, so it had been much longer than he'd thought. He felt a tug on his arm and rolled over, dragging Marisol along with him. It was only then that he remembered the handcuffs.

"Wake up," she muttered. "And get me out of these things."

"No," Ian said. "Go back to sleep."

"What do you think you're doing? You can't handcuff us together."

"I can and I did," Ian said.

"It—it's against the law. It's…kidnapping or—or unlawful something or other. I could call the police."

"I am the police, and if anyone asks, I'll just tell them it was kinky sex gone a bit awry. Now, go back to sleep."

She yanked on his arm again, forcing him to roll over and face her. She sat cross-legged on the bed, her hair tousled around her face, her color high. She'd never looked quite so beautiful and if this is what bondage did for her, then Ian was going to have to try it again.

"What do you expect to accomplish by this?" she asked, holding up her hand.

His arm dangled from hers and Ian grinned. "To keep you in my bed a little longer," he said.

"Why?"

"So we can talk," he replied. "You have some things to tell me and I'm not going to let you go until I have some answers to my questions. When I get those answers, I'll unlock the cuffs and you can go home."

"I thought you didn't want to know," she said.

He reached out with his free hand and stroked her cheek. "Now I do. I'm not going to pretend I don't care about you, Marisol, because I do. And whatever you say to me won't change how I feel. You have to trust me."

She groaned then curled up beside him and buried her face against his shoulder. "Just let me go home."

"You said you aren't doing anything illegal, so why can't you tell me?"

"Why not ask your brother? He's the one who dug up all the dirt."

"I want to hear it from you."

A long silence grew between them and Ian wondered if she were actually considering his request. He'd told her it wouldn't make a difference, that it wouldn't change his feelings for her. But did he really know that? What if she told him something so shocking it changed everything?

"You have to promise you won't interfere," she whispered. "Promise me."

Ian shook his head. "I can't. I won't. If there's any chance you might get hurt, I'm going to interfere."

She sat up, her hair falling around her face. Tears of frustration pushed at the corners of her eyes but she angrily brushed them away. "I want you to forget you're a cop, just for the next five minutes. Just be the man I'm sleeping with and nothing more."

"All right," Ian said.

"What would you do, if someone you knew, someone you loved, had committed a crime?"

"Did you commit a crime?" Ian asked.

She blinked in surprise and stared at him for a long moment. Only then, did he realize what he'd implied. Was he in love with Marisol? Is that why this was bothering him so? He shook his head. "So, we're speaking hypothetically?"

She nodded. "And suppose, your brother or your father, knew he'd made a mistake and he just wanted to fix it. No one has been hurt, it's a—a—"

"A victimless crime?" Ian asked.

Marisol nodded. "Yes, I suppose."

"Every crime has a victim," Ian said.

"I'm sure you'd see it that way, but sometimes it's not that way at all. I'm just trying to help straighten things out. To make things right so everyone will be happy."

"For the person you love?"

She nodded.

Ian drew a deep breath, knowing what his next question would cost him. "For David Barnett?"

Marisol frowned. "No, for my father."

"Then you're not in love with David Barnett?"

"Of course not. He's the one who got my father into this whole thing. I hate him. He's—he's self-absorbed and egotistical and condescending and he thinks he can do anything he wants without any consequences."

Ian lay back on the pillows, a flood of relief washing over him. He chuckled softly. She wasn't in love with David Barnett. She didn't even like him. So just what was she hiding from him? "He got you into this trouble? Maybe I can help you get out."

"Are you still the guy I'm sleeping with or are you a cop now?"

Ian pulled Marisol into his arms, molding her naked body to his, then kissed her forehead. "I'm the guy who cares about you."

Over the next hour, as the sun slowly rose, Marisol told him the whole story, about her father and his past, about David Barnett's scheme to sell forged paintings and about her rather risky plan to exchange the original for the forgery hanging in the Templetons' library using one of her own paintings as a decoy. And when she finished, Ian was certain of only one thing. He was completely in love with Marisol Arantes and he'd do whatever it took to protect her.

"You can't take the painting back," he said. "It's too risky. If you get caught, you'll be in as much trouble as your father."

"There is no other way. Not without involving my father. He's a convicted art forger. If he gets caught again, he'll probably spend the rest of his life in prison."

"All right," Ian said. "There has to be another way. I need a little time to think about it. Just don't do anything rash." He paused. "Where is the painting now?"

She smiled. "I shouldn't tell you."

Ian raised an eyebrow. "But you will."

"It's under your bed," she said.

He stared at her in disbelief. "What?"

"I brought it over here the other night and left it in the kitchen. After you were asleep I put it under the bed. It seemed like the safest place and David would never think to look here. By the way, there's a lot of dust under there. You really should vacuum once in a while."

"So now I am in the middle of this, right along with you?"

"I'm sorry," she murmured. "I didn't know what else to do. And I wasn't going to tell you, so if you hadn't handcuffed us together, you would have never known."

"And you just planned to keep sleeping with me until it came time to retrieve the painting?"

"I wasn't using you," she insisted. "Believe it or not, I like sleeping with you—and all the other stuff, too."

Ian laughed. "Do not try to sweet-talk me."

"If you want, I'll take the painting back to the gallery. You can forget it was ever there."

"No," he said. "Barnett tried to get it once. Who's to say he won't try again? I want the painting here and I want you here. I don't trust him, Marisol. He's got himself in deep shit and a man like him can get desperate. If he goes down, he's going to take you and your father with him. We have to figure out a way to stop that."

"We?" she asked.

Ian nodded. "We. You and I."

A smile curled the corners of her mouth. "I like the way that sounds."

Ian rolled on top of her, pressing his hips against hers, his shaft hard between them. "And I like the way you feel," he teased. "All soft and sweet." He nuzzled her neck. "Promise me you won't do anything until you give me a chance to help you. Maybe I can work something out."

"I promise," she said, giggling. "Do you think you can unlock the handcuffs now?"

"No way. I'm keeping you in this bed as long as I want. In fact, I may just call in and take a day off."

"Are you sure this isn't against the law?" Marisol asked.

"Yes," he murmured, kissing her neck. "But what I'm about to do to you just might be."

8

IAN STOOD at the conference table in Declan's office, staring at the painting he'd pulled from beneath his bed. It wasn't much to look at, at least not compared to Marisol's paintings. This seemed like a bunch of splotches on canvas.

All this fuss for something a kid might have painted. Though he'd learned to appreciate fine art, he still didn't understand why it was worth so damn much. After all, this was maybe thirty dollars worth of materials. A nice car had more in it in parts, yet sold for a lot less.

"Two hundred and fifty thousand dollars."

Both Ian and Declan stared in disbelief at Richard Christiansen, an art expert Declan had called in to meet with them. "What?" Ian gasped.

"Two hundred and fifty thousand," Christiansen repeated. "If it were an original Emory Colter. But it's not."

"Of course not," Ian muttered, covering his surprise. "What would I be doing with a painting worth that much?"

Dec watched from nearby, his gaze darting back and forth between Christiansen and the painting, his mind obviously intent on figuring out what was going on.

"What can you tell us about it?" Dec asked.

The expert bent over the painting and examined it through a magnifying glass. "Where did you get this?"

"I'm afraid I can't tell you that," Ian replied. "It's part of an ongoing police investigation."

The elderly man stepped back and rubbed his goatee thoughtfully. "Well, it's definitely a forgery. A very clever forgery."

"How do you know?"

"I'm quite familiar with Colter's work. In fact, I knew him very well before he died. He spent his summers in Newport and did some of his finest work there. I don't want to brag, but I'm considered the leading expert on Colter's early work."

Ian smiled tightly. He'd asked Dec to find him an art expert, and as always, Dec had known exactly who to call. Leave it to him to find the one guy who just might ask too many questions along with the answers he provided.

"You know, it's funny, but I was called upon to authenticate this very painting just last year. I couldn't. I was out of the country."

"So, you're sure this is a forgery?" Ian asked.

Christiansen nodded. "Although I can't tell you whoever did the painting had malicious intentions. Some collectors, especially corporations, have a copy done and they hang that in their corporate offices. The insurance is simply too high to put a valuable painting in a place that isn't as secure as a museum. The public gets to enjoy what they believe is an original while the original is tucked away in a vault for investment purposes. I can't say I approve of the practice, but it is done."

"So who could do work like this?" Ian asked.

"There's a number of artists. Do you want the artists operating on the right or the wrong side of the law?" he asked.

"Start with the wrong," Dec said.

"No," Ian interrupted. "I really don't need to know. All I wanted was to learn if the painting was an original. I have my answer."

"Ah, yes, well back to that. I'm afraid there's more. In most cases, the insurance company will take a photo of the borders for comparison when determining provenance and authenticity."

"The borders?" Ian asked.

"The edges. When a painting is framed, the public can't see the border. These are also hidden from view if the painting is reproduced or photographed. However, if the forger is in the presence of the real painting or a photo of the unframed painting, then a comparison of the borders is useless. In my opinion, this forger, or copyist, if you will, was working from the real painting, which might lead one to believe this had been commissioned by the owner of the painting."

"So how can you tell it's a forgery?" Dec asked.

"Because I have one bit of knowledge other appraisers don't. It's something Emory Colter told me long ago, something he always adds to each of his paintings, so he himself can recognize an original from a copy."

"What's that?" Ian asked.

"I can't tell you. If I did, I wouldn't be the foremost expert on Emory Colter. Suffice it to say I am positive this is not an original Emory Colter. I'd stake my reputation on it."

"What is it worth?" Ian asked.

"Maybe three or four thousand," he said. "Whatever the commission was and a good reproduction doesn't come cheap. However, if you do decide to sell it, you should —"

"Sell it?"

"Yes. If you plan to sell it, you must make sure the copy was authorized by the artist or his estate. If Emory Colter sold the reproduction rights to that painting, the owner can make all the copies he wants and it doesn't break the law. If someone other than the owner makes a copy, that's a different story."

Ian reached out and shook the elderly man's hand. "Thank you. I appreciate your help. I'd ask you keep this information confidential. This is an ongoing investigation."

"Of course, of course. I'm a bit of a crime buff myself. Always fancied I'd make a good detective. You will let me know what this was all about after you've arrested the perps, won't you?"

Ian held back a chuckle. "Yes, after we catch the perps, I'll be sure to call you."

Dec showed the appraiser out of the office and, a few moments later, returned with a grim expression on his face. "Are you going to tell me what this is all about?"

"That guy watches too many cop shows. The perps? I usually just call them the suspects. Skells, perps, scumbags. Makes them sound so glamorous. They're criminals."

"Speaking of criminals, where did you get that painting?" Dec held up his hand. "Never mind, I can guess where you got it. Why did you bring it here?"

"I needed to know what it was," Ian murmured. With a frustrated groan, he rubbed his eyes with his hands. "Just give me a moment or two to think this out."

Everything that he thought he knew had suddenly been turned upside down. Marisol intended to switch the original for the forgery. But she was in possession of the forgery, so that could only mean, she was after the original. Unless, she wasn't aware that the painting in her possession was the forgery. Perhaps, she thought it was the original.

"Did you get this from Marisol—"

Ian looked up. "Don't. The less you know, the better. I'm already in deeper than I care to be."

"I read the file. I know that Hector Arantes was convicted of art forgery and served ten years. He's out of prison now, and from the looks of things, he's up to his old tricks again. But how you got one of his forgeries, well…I figure his daughter must be mixed up in this. And you're mixed up with his daughter." Dec chuckled. "I saw the photo in the file. She's beautiful, I'll give her that."

"I'm not mixed up with her. Do you really think I'd be stupid enough to get involved with someone I suspect is breaking the law?"

Dec considered the question, then shook his head. "No," he finally said. "If I know one thing about you, Ian, you follow the rules, to the letter. So how did you get the painting?"

"She hid it, I borrowed it. I had to check it out for myself. I just didn't expect it to be a copy."

"You thought it was the original?"

Ian nodded. "She said it was. I guess either she was lying to me or she doesn't really know."

"You'd better find out." Dec clapped him on the back, then walked over to a low cabinet set against the wall. He opened a door to reveal a small refrigerator, then pulled out two bottles of orange juice, tossing one in Ian's direction. "So, why don't you tell me about the girl," he suggested.

Ian took a slow sip of the cold juice. "Wouldn't that be against the rules of your little game?"

"My game? I thought it was your game."

"No, as I recall, you were the one who suggested the celibacy pact. Three months, no women. Three months is a long time."

"I should be the one who is worried, don't you think? Marcus is stuck on a boat, eating organic mangoes and drinking champagne. You're chasing after a woman who might just be a criminal. Neither one of you is getting any."

"And you are?" Ian asked.

"No," Dec replied. "I'm spending all my time trying to find Trevor Ross's runaway daughter, Eden. It seems she got herself into a little mess in Europe and now her daddy is going to have to bail her out. I went out to talk to Marcus earlier this week, hoping he might have seen her hanging around Ross's estate, but he's completely useless when it comes to doing my legwork."

"He's a creative type," Ian commented. "They think a lot differently than you and me."

Declan gave him a skeptical look, then shook his head. "Why don't we go out and get some lunch? I know we're supposed to get together at your place tonight, but since you're here, we can call Marcus and hang out here in Providence."

Ian glanced at his watch, the took another gulp of the orange juice. "I have to get back," he said. "But thanks for taking care of this so quickly. And let me know what I owe you for the art expert."

"I'm sure my company can cover his fees. I'll see you tonight," he called as Ian walked to the door.

"Yeah, right," Ian said. "Tonight. My place."

When he reached the parking ramp beneath Dec's office building, he sat in his car for a long time, trying to figure out his next move. He was usually an excellent judge of character, knowing immediately when someone was lying to him. But his radar was off when it came to Marisol. He could never really focus when he was with her. Her beauty, her sensuality, became a distraction, clouding his brain until he could barely think.

If she was aware she had the forgery, then he could assume she was working with David Barnett. If not, then perhaps she was being used by Barnett. So did he treat her as an unwitting accomplice or a full-fledged conspirator?

The only way he'd know for sure was to confront her, which he intended to do the moment he returned to Bonnett Harbor.

"IT'S PERFECT," Marisol said, holding up Sascha's Balenciaga bag. "See, you can't even tell what's inside."

They sat at the worktable in the rear of Gallerie Luna, sipping on cold glasses of limeade and eating shortbread cookies. Sascha had arrived from New York just that morning, determined to convince Marisol to give the painting back to her father and be done with it.

But no amount of convincing, even Sascha's whining, would change Marisol's mind. The more she considered her plan, the better she thought it would work. She'd promised Ian she'd give him a chance to fix everything, but he didn't deserve to be dragged into this. She could do it on her own.

"I know this will work," Marisol said. It had to. And the sooner, the better.

Sascha toyed with a tube of paint. "I'm starting to get nervous. What if something goes wrong? Shouldn't we practice? How do I know throwing this in the sink will knock out the alarm system? How do I know I won't electrocute myself?"

"Just don't touch the water," Marisol said. "And make sure it's on before you toss it in. Did you call the

Templetons? Remember, we have to be there in daylight, or I won't have light to work."

"I did," Sascha replied. "And we've been invited over for brunch on Sunday. You're lucky they love your work. She was hoping we'd join her for cocktails this evening, but I said we were busy."

"But we aren't," Marisol said. "Why didn't you accept?"

"Because I didn't think we were ready." Sascha fanned her face with her hand. "I have to prepare myself. I've never broken the law." She paused, frowning. "Well, not any big laws. I did smoke pot when I was in college. And of course, I never drive the speed limit. And I once took a parking ticket from my car and put it on another car."

"I'm sorry I put you in this situation," Marisol said. "You're a good friend to do this for me. I don't know how I'll ever pay you back."

"With many large commissions," Sascha said. "After this, you're going to get back to work and we're going to plan your opening. I have some important clients I intend to invite and they're going to be spending obscene amounts of money on your work."

Marisol smiled. "Good. I'm going to need obscene amounts of money if I intend to settle here. I can't live in that tiny apartment upstairs much longer."

"Settle here?" Sascha asked. "You can't be serious. This was supposed to be a summer place for you. In the winter, you go back to the city."

"I was thinking I'd live here full-time. I'm not that far from New York and it's quiet here and—"

"Don't do this," Sascha warned. "Don't throw yourself into another relationship so soon after David. I know this policeman is handsome, but what could you two possibly have in common?"

"He's the police chief," she said, gathering her patience. "And we have plenty in common." Sascha was her friend, and a business partner, but there were times when she acted like Marisol's mother.

Sascha stood up and paced back and forth between the worktable and the sofa. "You belong in the city. Everyone who is anyone is lives in the city. You need to be seen, at parties and gallery openings. People will forget."

"There are plenty of successful artists who live outside New York City."

"Of course. But they all have established careers and a solid market for their work. You're not there yet."

Marisol got up from the worktable and walked back to the kitchen to fetch the pitcher of limeade. She refilled Sascha's glass, then sat down on her stool. "I'm not just staying for him," she said.

"You aren't?"

"Maybe I am," Marisol admitted. "But what's wrong with that? I want to see where this all leads. We have this incredible chemistry. When we're together he can't keep his hands off me. I've never had that with a man before. Do you know how good it feels to be desired like that?"

"What about David?"

"No," Marisol said. "This is different. With David,

everything was so predictable. We were the perfect couple, but he didn't want me. Not the way Ian does."

"So this guy is good in bed," Sascha said. "How good could he be?"

Marisol smiled slyly. "Very, very good. No, unbelievably great. Fabulous. I don't know. There isn't really an adjective to describe it. It's just—wow!"

"Magnificent? Astonishing? Extraordinary?" Sascha prompted.

"All of those. And really, really hot. Intense. And his body is just to die for."

Sascha sighed as she plopped back down on her stool. "Every woman's dream man?"

"Yeah," Marisol said.

They silently stared across the room at the painting she'd done of Ian, both of them lost in their own thoughts. When the front buzzer sounded, they both looked toward the door.

"I suppose that's him," Sascha said.

"Can you give us a minute?"

She nodded, grabbed her bag and walked to the back of the gallery. Marisol hurried to the door and pulled it open, expecting to see Ian. But David stood outside.

When she tried to slam the door, he stuck his foot inside, then shoved the door so hard, she had to step back. He stalked into the gallery, letting the door slam behind him. Slowly, he took in the paintings and the sculptures scattered around the room.

"Where is it?" he muttered. "I want the painting. I know you have it."

"I don't know what you're talking about," Marisol said. "Just leave, David."

"Your father sent you the Colter. I need it. And if you don't give it to me, I'm going to let the authorities know your father is back to his old tricks again."

"I don't know what you're talking about," Marisol repeated.

He spun around and grabbed her arms, his fingers biting into her flesh. "I have a buyer who wants his painting. If I don't give it to him, he's going to be very angry. He might just decide to hurt me."

"Then I guess you shouldn't have gotten involved with him," Marisol said.

"Tell me where it is," he muttered.

"Go ahead," Marisol said. "Search the place. I don't know where it is or where my father is. I haven't heard from him in weeks. And if he is involved in some scheme with you, then I don't want to hear about it. He's an adult, he makes his own choices. And I've made mine. Look for your damn painting and then get out, before I call the police."

"Marisol?" Sascha slowly walked toward them, her eyes fixed on David. "Is everything all right?"

"Yes, fine."

"Hello, David. You're looking…flushed. Are you feeling all right?"

"Yes, fine," he replied.

"Well, then, we're all fine. Can I get you something to drink?"

David shook his head. "Would you excuse us? Marisol and I have important matters to discuss."

"I'll just be in the back," she said, "in case I'm needed."

When Sascha had disappeared, David grabbed Marisol again and cursed beneath his breath. But this time, she yanked out of his grasp, crossing her arms in front of her.

"Find your father and convince him to bring back my painting. Or all the trouble that's going to rain down on me is going to come down on him, too. And you."

"I'll see if I can find him," Marisol said, keeping her tone cool and indifferent. "I'll call you."

He nodded curtly, then turned for the door.

"David?" Her voice stopped him and he faced her. In three short strides she was in front of him. Without thinking, she drew her hand back and slapped his face, the sound echoing through the silence of the gallery.

"You can't protect your father," he said.

"That wasn't for my father. That was for me. For making me believe I didn't deserve anything more than you gave me. I know differently now."

He opened his mouth to reply, then thought better of it and turned on his heel, stalking to the door. A few moments later, it slammed behind him and Marisol released a tightly held breath. "We can't wait," she called.

Sascha appeared by her side. "Wait for what?"

"We're going now. To the Templetons'."

"We can't," Sascha said.

"You said she wanted us there for cocktails. Well, call her and tell her we can make it. And we're coming right now. We just have to pick up the painting from Ian's place and we'll be on our way. After we switch them, I'm going to give the forgery to David and he can give that to his buyer. Hopefully, that will be enough to appease him."

"Maybe we should wait and think this out a bit," Sascha said.

But Marisol was through thinking about this. She needed to grab this opportunity now and solve her problem, instead of worrying over it for the next day and a half. As she dragged her decoy painting toward the back of the gallery, she tossed Sascha her car keys. "Bring your car around to the back. And don't forget the heat gun."

After struggling to fit the crate in the back of Sascha's Volvo wagon, they finally wedged it in and slammed the hatch shut. Then Marisol ran back inside to grab the tools she'd packed in her favorite bag. When she was settled inside the car, she took a deep breath.

"I can see why art thieves do what they do," she said. "It's kind of a rush, all this excitement and nerves. Will we get caught, won't we get caught, who knows—"

"Shut up," Sascha said as she started the car. "Let's not talk or I'm going to get out of this car and walk back to New York."

"All right," Marisol said. "No talking. Just drive."

Marisol directed Sascha through the streets of Bonnett Harbor, watching carefully to see if they were being followed. She wouldn't put it past David to be lurking in the shadows, watching her every move. But after taking a circuitous route through town, she decided that David had retreated to lick his wounds and revise his strategy.

"Turn down this street," she said. Sascha drove to the middle of the block, then Marisol pointed to Ian's house. "I'm going to go inside and get the painting. Circle the block a couple times and I'll run out. If you see anyone on the street, don't slow down, just keep going."

"We should be doing this at night," Sascha said. "Not in broad daylight."

"Well, we don't have a choice." Marisol hopped out of the car, glanced both ways and ran up the driveway to the side door. She grabbed the doorknob and turned it, but to her surprise, the door wouldn't open.

"No," she moaned. "It can't be locked." Frantically, she pulled up the mat and searched for a key. She couldn't blame Ian for locking the house, considering the valuable painting under his bed. Or maybe he'd done it to prevent her from retrieving the painting without his knowledge.

Marisol walked around the back of the house, then noticed a window open in the breakfast nook. She grabbed a lawn chair and pulled it over to the house, balancing on it as she tore off the screen. A few moments later, she raised the sash and crawled inside.

She raced upstairs and found the painting where she'd left it. Dragging it from beneath the bed, Marisol tucked it under her arm and hurried back outside, this time using the kitchen door. She saw Sascha circle the block, then waited for her to appear again before running out to the street.

When she was safely inside the car, Marisol

screamed, unable to control her nerves. Then, a laugh erupted and she couldn't seem to stop the emotions bubbling to the surface. She wasn't happy or amused or even frustrated. She was just scared.

"Are you all right?" Sascha asked.

"I will be," she said. "Once this is all over."

"FIRST OFF, YOU CAN'T TALK to women, so how can you be honest with them? They have no capacity for logical reasoning. They're driven by emotions. Let me tell you, getting into a real conversation with a woman is like stepping on a land mine. One stupid move, one offhand comment or misplaced adjective and, boom, you're dead."

Ian waited for his brothers to respond, knowing what he'd said was complete bullshit. At one time, he believed that women were incapable of logical thought. But then he'd met Marisol. He didn't have to work hard to figure her out. She was just…Marisol.

"And you can't depend upon women," Declan commented. "They may have your back now, but the minute you don't agree with them, they'll cut your legs out from under you. You want someone who'll have your back? That's what brothers are for."

"Women are not the enemy," Marcus said.

Ian stared at Marcus for a long moment, grinning. "Did *you* break the pact?"

"No!" Marcus said. "I've just figured out a few things for myself."

"So, are you planning to share with us?" Declan asked.

Marcus shook his head. "Not at the moment."

A long silence descended on the group as Ian and Dec stood at the grill and stared into the fire. Ian dumped a bit of beer onto the flames that licked at the burgers. He listened distractedly as Dec and Marcus discussed the search for Eden Ross, but his mind kept wandering to Marisol.

"Louise Wilson over at the diner mentioned there were a couple of guys wandering around Bonnett Harbor asking if anyone had seen her," Ian commented. "They're promising a big payday for information. Ten thousand for a tip that leads to a photo of Eden Ross. I'm thinking I ought to be out looking for her."

"She must be close by, then," Dec said.

"Why do you say that?" Marcus asked.

Ian walked over to the picnic table and grabbed another beer from the cooler, taking the chance to glance at his watch. Dinner would be ready in a few minutes, a half hour to eat, another half hour to hang out and he could be over at Marisol's by six or six-thirty.

"I gotta go," Marcus said.

Ian frowned. "You haven't had anything to eat."

Marcus shrugged. "The wind is supposed to pick up later tonight and I've got to set another anchor."

"So how's the job going for you?" Dec called. "What did Ross think about the work?"

"He thought it was great," Marcus yelled.

"He's an odd one, that boy," Declan said, staring after their younger brother.

"I can never quite figure what's going on in his

head," Ian commented. "You really think he's found himself a girl?"

"Nah," Dec said. "All Marcus cares about is his work. Besides, who would he meet staying out on the boat?"

They sat outside for the next hour, enjoying their dinner and chatting about work. Ian avoided talking about Marisol and the painting, and instead, pumped Dec for information on Eden Ross. In the end, Dec enlisted Ian's help in the search, asking him to keep an eye out for Eden, as well.

He finally left at seven and Ian hurried upstairs to change out of his uniform, pulling on a fresh T-shirt and a pair of jeans. He noticed the covers on the bed had been tossed back, and smoothed them in place with his hand. Slowly, Ian realized someone had been in his bedroom.

He dropped to the floor and peered under the bed. "Oh, hell," he muttered. The painting was gone. And it didn't take a rocket scientist to know who had it. She must have been here before he returned home from work. He tugged on a pair of Nikes, tucked his badge in the back pocket of his jeans, then raced downstairs.

If Marisol had any thought to switch those paintings tonight, then it might already be too late. He jumped into his car and threw it in gear, backing down the driveway and swinging the Mustang out into the street.

A few minutes later, he pulled up in front of Gallerie Luna. Marisol's car was parked out front, but she wasn't answering the buzzer. For a brief moment, he felt a prickle of panic, then decided that there was no need to jump to conclusions. Maybe she'd gone for a walk, maybe she was waiting for him at his house right now.

He tried the buzzer once more, then returned to his car, double-parked in front of the gallery. He'd just take a drive over to Newport and check in with the Templetons. And if she wasn't there, he'd put out an APB on her and have the rest of the Bonnett Harbor police force helping in the search.

As he sped across the Newport Bridge, his thoughts returned to the meeting in Declan's office. Though he didn't want to believe the worst in Marisol, there was a tiny voice that told him she could be lying about the painting. For all he knew, she was aware that the painting in her possession was a fake and her intention all along was to steal the real painting. Hell, she could be working with David Barnett on this scheme.

The gates to the Templeton mansion were open when he approached on Ruggles Avenue. He parked on the circular drive and turned off the car. But as soon as the engine stopped, he heard a loud siren sounding from inside the house. "The burglar alarm," he murmured. Maybe he was too late?

He grabbed his badge from his pocket, then jogged up to the front door. Ian rang the bell once, then opened the door. Cheryl Templeton stood in the foyer, her hands pressed to her ears as he held out his badge.

"Oh, thank God you're here. I can't remember the code to the system. The security company is on the phone and they won't switch off the alarm until I give them the code." She held out the phone. "You talk to them."

"Where is your husband?"

"He's out of town on business," she said. "Please, tell them they can turn off the alarm. Why aren't you wearing your uniform?"

"I'm undercover," Ian said. She seemed to accept the answer, to Ian's relief. "Is there anyone else in the house?"

"Yes. Sascha Duroy is here and Marisol Arantes. Marisol was in the library and I'm not sure where Sascha is."

"Let me check around first," he said, taking the phone from her hand. "Why don't you wait out front, just for your own safety. When I find the other two ladies, I'll send them out. And once the house is clear, I'll tell the security company to turn off the alarm."

"Tell them the power went off and that's what set off the alarm. There aren't any burglars."

Ian waited until Cheryl Templeton was outside, then tried the library door, but found it locked. Cursing, he rapped sharply. "Marisol!" He knocked again. "Marisol, let me in."

A moment later, the door swung open. She reached out and grabbed him, then dragged him inside. "What are you doing here?"

"The question is, what are *you* doing here?"

"I don't have time for this," she muttered. "Did anyone see you come in? How did you get in the house? Where is Mrs. Templeton?"

"Mrs. Templeton let me in. She's under the

impression I'm responding to their security alert. I don't think she realized I'm not the Newport police."

Marisol hurried back to the painting on the wall, grasping the frame as she tried to lift it off the hook. "You could give me a hand here. I don't have much time. Did you lock the door behind you?"

Ian grabbed his handcuffs and snapped one side on her left wrist, then reached across and caught her right. She didn't realize what he was doing until she couldn't move her arms.

"This is no time for games!" she cried above the alarm "Take these things off me."

"Not until you look me in the eye and tell me what you're really doing here. I know the truth, Marisol."

"Of course you do. I told you."

He grabbed her hands and forced her to face him, looking deeply into her eyes, watching the emotions play across her expression. She looked frightened and frantic. "The painting on the wall is the real one," he said.

Her eyes went wide and she gasped. In that moment, Ian knew she had no knowledge of what was really going on. "But it can't be. How do you know?"

"I took the one hidden under my bed to an expert this morning. He verified it was a forgery. He knew Emory Colter. He was sure, Marisol. You were going to replace the real painting with the fake."

She fell back in the chair as the revelation sank in. "And then I was going to give David the fake. But it would have been the real painting. And I would have never known." She paused. "Why did you handcuff me?"

"Because I wasn't sure whether you knew or not."

"Of course I didn't know. How could you think—" She paused, anger flashing in her eyes. "Get me out of these."

He unlocked the cuffs. "Straighten things up in here. I'm going to get the alarm switched off. Where is Sascha?"

"In the bathroom. Blowing out the electricity."

"Can you do this?"

Marisol nodded. "Just go."

Ian turned for the door, holding the phone up to his ear. "This is Police Captain Ian Quinn from the Bonnett Harbor Police Department. I'm a guest here at Mrs. Templeton's. My badge number is 743. I'm checking the house now."

He made a cursory search of the mansion, knowing there weren't any burglars. He found Sascha standing outside the powder room beneath the stairs, water dripping from her oversize handbag. "I think you better go out front and wait for me."

She nodded, then brushed by him, avoiding his gaze. He walked through the first floor of the house, then peeked back inside the library. Marisol was standing next to the fireplace, her painting propped up against the mahogany desk.

"All set?"

Marisol nodded, joining him at the library door. "Thank you," she murmured.

He took her hand and led her outside. "The house is clear," Ian said into the phone. A few moments later, the alarm switched off, leaving Ian with ringing ears.

"Oh, thank you," Mrs. Templeton said. "I'm so glad you

came." She frowned. "How did you get here so quickly? The alarm just went off a few seconds before you arrived."

"I actually came to help Marisol," he said. "But I got delayed. I understand she has a gift for you."

Cheryl Templeton clapped her hands. "Yes. I can hardly wait. Can we see it?"

"Maybe we should get the power turned on first?" Ian suggested.

"Oh, I put the gardener on that task." She grabbed Sascha by the arm, then caught Marisol's hand. "Are we ready? Can I see it now? Come along, let's go."

Ian followed the trio back inside the house and waited at the library door. Cheryl Templeton covered her eyes as Sascha led her inside and Marisol stood next to her painting. She nodded at Ian and he quickly moved to the crate, grabbing it and taking it out the door while Mrs. Templeton still had her eyes covered.

"Are you ready?" Marisol asked as Ian closed the door behind him.

He carried the crate to Sascha's car and slid it into the back. As he slammed the hatch, Ian sighed, satisfied that he'd done all he could to keep Marisol and her father out of jail—for now. But there was still one wild card in this whole mess and that was David Barnett.

Barnett was short a painting and as long as he believed Marisol had the Colter, he wouldn't leave her alone. Since Ian didn't have a reason to arrest him, something else had to be done. But what?

Ian glanced up as Marisol and Sascha hurried out of the house, offering their apologies for such a hasty exit.

Cheryl Templeton followed after them, imploring everyone to stay for dinner. But to Ian's relief, the invitation was graciously refused.

Sascha got into the Volvo and Marisol grabbed for the passenger's door, but Ian took her elbow and steered her toward the Mustang. "You're coming with me," he said.

"I—I should go with Sascha. She has the painting."

Ian shook his head. "I'm not letting you out of my sight again until we've decided what to do with that damned painting."

Marisol slid into the Mustang and Ian hurried around to the driver's side. They followed Sascha down the driveway and once out of sight of the house, he glanced over at Marisol.

She sent him a weak smile. "Sorry?"

Ian laughed. "Sorry? Do you realize what would have happened had you actually made that switch? That was theft, Marisol. You could have ended up in prison for a very long time."

She opened her mouth to speak, but Ian held up his hand. Right now, he wasn't interested in explanations. This certainly wasn't what he was taught at the police academy, nor had his ten years of job experience prepared him to dance along the edges of the law as he had tonight.

The only consolation was that, for the moment, Marisol was on the right side of the law—his side.

9

MARISOL STOOD BENEATH the shower in Ian's bathroom, hot water pouring over her head, washing away the last of the tension that had plagued her for days.

After they'd left the Templetons', they'd all met up at Ian's house, returning the painting to the hiding place beneath his bed. She'd been shaken by how close she'd come to committing a real crime and furious at how she'd nearly been duped into giving David the real painting. But Ian had poured her a glass of wine, and for the next hour, they'd sat in his backyard and talked, the conversation slowly calming her.

Ian had made it clear what he thought needed to be done. The forgery ought to be destroyed and David Barnett hung out to dry. But Marisol insisted on keeping the painting, knowing that David would never let the matter rest until he had something to sell to his collector.

Marisol reached for the soap, then felt Ian's hands on her waist. "What are you doing in here?" she asked, smiling back at him.

"I thought you might need some help," he said. Ian reached up and gently massaged her shoulders.

She turned and faced him, wrapping her arms around his neck. "I've always liked you naked," she teased, "but naked and wet is even nicer."

"Are you all right?" he asked.

Marisol nodded. She hadn't told Ian about her plans to give the painting to David. Technically, that action would probably put her on the wrong side of the law again, but she didn't care. She was simply giving the painting back to the man who paid for it.

"I'm going to sleep so well tonight," she said.

"You'll need your rest," Ian said. "You have a big day tomorrow."

"We're sleeping in tomorrow," she said. "It's Saturday."

"We have business down at the station," Ian said, running his fingers through her wet hair.

Marisol frowned. "What business?"

"With the FBI. I'm going to call them in to deal with David Barnett."

Marisol gasped. "What? You can't do that. I'm going to give him the painting and he's going to leave me and my father alone."

"David Barnett is a criminal," Ian said. "I did a little checking and Barnett is under investigation. This isn't the first piece of artwork he's tried to pass off as an original. It's time he was stopped and we have the opportunity to do that."

Marisol shook her head, then stepped out of the shower. How dare he make a decision like this without consulting her? He had no right, even if he was the police chief of Bonnett Harbor. This was her father's life they were talking about, not some faceless criminal who deserved jail time.

She grabbed a towel and wrapped it around her body, her hair dripping water on the floor. "No," she said as he followed her out of the shower. "I'm not going to do it. When they find out my father made that forgery, they'll arrest him again."

Ian grabbed her arms and met her gaze. "If you help them, you can make a deal for your father," he said. "As long as we stop Barnett from selling that painting, then what your father did was a copyright violation at best. He'll get a slap on the wrist and nothing more. But if Barnett sells that painting, then your father is part of the conspiracy. Do you understand?"

Marisol looked into Ian's eyes, searching for the truth in his words. She'd trusted him once and he'd helped her. She had to trust him again. "But how will we do this?" she said. "Don't I have to tell them what he did?"

"No," Ian said. "I have a plan."

Marisol moaned, shaking her head. "Not another plan. I can't do another plan. I like my plan. It's so simple. Call David, give him the painting. One, two, it's over."

"It won't be difficult," he assured her. "I'll be with you the whole way. It will be the right thing to do."

"What is the FBI going to say when they find out the police chief of Bonnett Harbor has been sleeping with the daughter of an infamous art forger?"

"We're not going to tell them that part," Ian said.

"What are we going to tell them?"

He reached down and hooked her chin with his

finger, then kissed her gently. "We'll leave all that to later," he murmured. "I have other things on my mind right now."

"What?"

Ian traced a line along her shoulder, down her arm to her wrist. "I was thinking you might want to crawl into bed with me and see what happens?"

A tiny smile twitched at her lips. Things had changed between them. The trust between them had been tested and it had survived. And for the first time, she could see a future with Ian. She needed him, now more than ever. "I know what will happen," Marisol said, taking his hand and leading him to the bedroom.

"You're not going to let me sleep. You're going to keep me awake all night long. And tomorrow, I'm going to be too tired to talk to the FBI."

"Now there's a plan," she said.

"You don't think I can control myself?" Ian said. "I can have you in my bed and do nothing but sleep."

"Well, that would be a waste, wouldn't it?" Marisol asked.

"All right, let's see who has the most self-control." Ian grabbed the towel she'd wrapped around her and tugged it off her body. "Come on," he said as he dried himself with her towel. "Let's just go to bed and see who falls asleep first."

Marisol knew he was just teasing, but she decided to go along with the game. If he was determined to prove a point, then she'd do her best to disprove it. It wouldn't take more that a simple caress to shake his resolve.

She snatched the towel from his hands and dried her wet hair, then crawled into his bed. He lay down beside her, tugging the sheet up around his waist.

"See, no problem."

"You're not asleep yet," she said.

Marisol rolled over on her side and watched him, but Ian refused to look at her. "I see you're very determined." She held her hand over his chest, hovering just above his skin. "I won't touch you then." She ran her hand down, holding it over his crotch. Then, Marisol began to move her palm back and forth, as if she were stroking him.

It took no time at all for him to react, his growing erection pressing against the sheets. She smiled in satisfaction. "Oh, my. What could that be?"

With a low growl, Ian reached out and grabbed her, pulling her on top of him. "You are a bad, bad girl," he said.

"Just remember, you touched me first," she countered. "So I guess I win."

"Can I give you your prize now?" Ian asked.

Marisol giggled. This was what she loved about Ian, these moments when she could be completely herself, when the world fell away and it was just them. She was falling in love with him, and every day, the feelings simply grew stronger and stronger.

Bonnett Harbor was supposed to be a fresh start for her, a place to escape a relationship gone bad. But instead, it had been a destination, a place for her to find something special, something real. And maybe something lasting.

"DO YOU UNDERSTAND what to do if you feel your life is in danger, Miss Arantes?"

Ian watched from behind the one-way glass, his gaze fixed on Marisol's face. She was scared and he had serious doubts she'd heard anything the two FBI agents had said to her since they'd sat down in the small interview room earlier that afternoon. Her fingers kept fluttering to her throat, as she kept her eyes on the microphone set in front of her.

"David Barnett is a desperate man," the female agent explained. "We don't know how far he's willing to go to get what he wants. We believe the buyer waiting for this particular painting is a highly placed member of the Japanese mob. If Barnett doesn't deliver, then he'd be in serious danger."

"I—I don't think he would hurt me," Marisol said, looking up at Agent Phillips.

"But if he does try, what do you say?" Agent DiMarco asked.

She turned to the male agent. "I say, 'My father is a good man.' And then I wait for you to come in. When you do, I duck for cover as fast as possible."

"Good girl," Ian murmured to himself. But would she remember once she was alone with Barnett? Did she have the courage to pull this plan off? And did he have the fortitude to sit back and watch as she did it?

It had taken every ounce of his resolve to walk away from her, to leave her in the care of the two FBI agents. But he and Marisol had agreed on the story they would tell. It was the truth, they could both swear to it, although it wasn't the whole truth.

He'd convinced her of the strategy late last night, lying in bed with her wrapped in his arms. After she'd agreed, they'd carefully mapped out how they were going to make it work. Everything depended on Marisol reacting exactly as she should have the day she opened the painting.

Ian had left for the station early that morning, and an hour later, Sascha had arrived with her car. She and Marisol had loaded the painting and driven it to the Bonnett Harbor police station, where Ian had been waiting.

Like clockwork, Sally had called him from his office, announcing that Marisol Arantes was waiting in the lobby with a rather large crate. And from there, Ian did everything a good police chief would do. He interviewed Marisol, asked pointed questions about the painting and her father, checked out her facts and wrote his report. And then, right on schedule, he had called in the FBI.

Ian had expected to wait at least a day or two for a response, but to his surprise, the mention of David Barnett's name brought instant interest. Within three hours, two agents had arrived from the New York office, anxious to interview Marisol.

She'd been with them for almost two hours now and Ian could see exhaustion in every expression, in every movement. Agent DiMarco pushed back from the table and walked out of the room. A few seconds later, the door to the observation room opened. "We're going to go on this tonight," he said.

Ian gasped. "Tonight? Come on, you can see she's exhausted. Give her a chance to calm down and get some sleep. You can do it tomorrow."

Agent DiMarco shook his head. "The longer we wait, the more Barnett is going to suspect it's a setup. Her nervousness can work to our advantage. Agent Phillips is going to get her wired up and then we're going to have her call Barnett and ask him to meet her at the gallery."

"He's in town," Ian said.

Agent DiMarco frowned. "And you know this because?"

"When she mentioned his name in our interview, I figured I better find out where he was and what he was doing. So I put out an APB on his car. He's staying across the bay in Newport. I've got an unmarked car watching his room. If he leaves, we'll know about it."

"Good," Agent DiMarco said, smiling appreciatively. "I wish all local law enforcement was as thorough as you've been."

Ian felt a prickle of guilt at accepting the compliment. If the FBI had any idea what Ian really knew, he'd be in that interview room and the questions would not be friendly. In any other situation, Ian would question his ethics. But the fact was, Marisol hadn't been guilty of anything more than loving her father and wanting to protect him. And Ian hadn't been guilty of anything more than feeling the same toward Marisol. Going in, he knew the potential consequences if they were found out, but he was willing to risk his career for Marisol.

"I ordered something for her to eat," Ian said. "Can I take it to her?"

"Sure," DiMarco said. "We'll have her call Barnett and set up the meeting for 9:00 p.m. at her gallery. We'll take her back there and get her set up after she's eaten."

Ian grabbed the paper bag Sally had delivered from the diner and walked out of the observation room. He nodded at Agent Phillips as he passed her in the hallway, then heard Sally call him from the door of his office.

"There you are," she said. "I just wanted to let you know that Delaney and Wilson answered a call last night at the Sandpiper about a supposed car theft. Turns out Eden Ross was staying there."

Ian frowned. "Eden Ross?"

"Yes," Sally said. "Remember you told me to tell you if any of us heard anything about her? Well, she was—"

"Did Delaney and Wilson write up a report?"

Sally nodded. "It turns out that the car that was the object of the theft belonged to Trevor Ross and the suspected thieves were really tabloid photographers. We tracked the call through the motel switchboard and we're sure it came from her room."

"I don't have time for this now," Ian said. "Call Dec's cell phone an give him the info. He's the one who's looking for her."

Ian entered the interview room and sat down across the table from Marisol, his back to the mirrored window. Tears swam in Marisol's eyes as she gazed at him.

"They're probably watching us," he whispered. "And

listening." Ian pulled a can of soda pop from the bag, opened it and placed it in front of her. "How are you doing?"

"They knew all about David Barnett," she said. "They've been building a case against him. And they knew my father was involved. And they thought I was involved, too, because of my relationship with David." She took a quick sip of the soda. "If I help them, they promised not to prosecute my father."

Ian smiled, clutching his hands in front of him. "See, I told you everything would be all right." It took every ounce of his determination not to reach out and touch her. Her fingers trembled and he fought the urge to gather her hands in his and press them against his body. "You'll do fine. These agents know what they're doing. You'll be safe."

"Are you going to be there?"

"I don't know," Ian said. "I hope so."

"After I do this, it will be over, won't it?"

He nodded and smiled. "And then you can get on with your life."

"My life," she repeated. "What if they change their minds? What if David tells them my father—"

"It's all right. I heard them make the offer. Once you do this, there will be papers to sign. You won't have to worry, your father will be safe."

"The FBI thinks David's been running this scam for years, selling bogus art. He started out with small stuff, then gradually moved on to the more valuable pieces. My father will have to testify about the art he copied, but that should be the end of it. I'm not going to let them know where he is until everything is official," she said. "They can't make me."

A single tear trickled down her cheek and she brushed it away. Ian needed to take her into his arms, to soothe and protect her. He was the one who had talked her into this and now he was watching her crumble before his eyes.

"You'd tell me if they were trying to trick me, wouldn't you?"

He nodded, then shoved his chair back from the table. "You look like you could use some air, Miss Arantes," Ian said. "Would you like to step outside for a few minutes?" She shook her head, but Ian persisted. "Really. You look pale, Miss Arantes."

"I—I guess I could use some air," she finally said, meeting Ian's gaze. She stood up and Ian followed her out.

They passed Agent DiMarco in the hallway and Ian pulled him aside. "She's feeling a bit overwhelmed. I'm just going to take her out back for some fresh air. She'll be fine."

"I'll take her," DiMarco said.

Marisol held up her hand. "No, I'll be all right with Chief Quinn. I just need a moment to myself. I'm not going to run away."

Agent DiMarco considered her request for a long moment, then nodded. "Just for a few minutes. Then we need to go over a few more things and get you wired up."

Ian rested his hand on the small of Marisol's back as he steered her toward the back entrance of the police station. The rear parking area was fenced and completely hidden from the street. The moment the door closed behind them, he took her hand and pulled her over into the shadows. "Are you all right?" he murmured, cupping her face in his palms.

Marisol nodded. "I'm a little nervous. What if I can't do this? I've never been very good at lying."

Ian bent close, then kissed her, his fingers furrowing through her hair. It was the only way he knew to reassure her, and himself. She leaned into his body as his tongue delved into her mouth, so sweet and warm.

"It'll be all right," he whispered against her lips. "After it's over, it'll just be us again."

Those words seemed to calm her nerves and she surrendered herself to his kiss, wrapping her arms around his neck and pulling him closer. Ian's hands skimmed over her back and then circled her waist, lifting her up off her feet until her whole body was pressed against his.

"Take me away from here," Marisol pleaded. "I don't want to do this."

Ian drew back and looked down into her face, just barely illuminated by the lights from the nearby parking lot. "I will," he said. "If you really want me to, I will."

She blinked in surprise at his response. "But you'd get in trouble. Wouldn't you lose your job?"

"Maybe. I'd probably be arrested, too. But you're more important to me than my job."

"Don't say that," she murmured, shaking her head.

Marisol took a deep breath, then straightened. "I can do this. I'll be all right. You don't have to worry."

"And why can't I worry?" he asked, aware of the sudden distance between them. Why was she suddenly pushing him away?

"This is my problem and I'm the one responsible. I don't want you to bear any of the consequences."

"Damn it, Marisol, we're in this together now. The moment you told me the truth, it became our problem."

"And this is exactly why I didn't want to tell you," she shouted, yanking out of his grasp. "I didn't want it to be your problem."

Ian cursed softly, leaning back against the brick wall of the station. "So what? Then I'm not allowed to care about you? This is what a relationship is about, Marisol. We help each other, we support each other. What's wrong with that?"

"Nothing," she murmured, refusing to meet his gaze.

He reached out and tipped her face up to his. "You're allowed to care about me," he said. "It's all right. This stopped being all about sex a long time ago. I think you know that but you're afraid to admit it."

"I—I should go back in," she said.

"Yes," Ian said. "You probably should."

She turned and hurried to the door. Ian faced the wall, bracing his hands over his head and drawing a deep breath of the warm night air. Maybe he wasn't supposed to care the way he did about Marisol, but he sure as hell couldn't stop himself.

He strode to the door, then paused before he opened

it. When this was all over, he planned to let Marisol know exactly how he felt about her. And if she still refused to see him as anything more than a lover, then he'd have to find a way to change her mind.

MARISOL'S HEART slammed in her chest as she reached for the lock on the gallery door, fighting back a surge of nerves. She resisted the temptation to glance back at the rear of the gallery where Agent DiMarco had hidden himself in the storage room. Outside, Ian and Agent Phillips were parked a half block away in an unmarked car, recording everything her microphone picked up.

She felt completely alone and vulnerable. In truth, she'd wanted Ian inside the gallery, but the FBI agents had said no. She reached for the door again, then drew a deep breath to calm her nerves. She'd only have one chance at this, once chance to make it all right, one chance at a future with Ian Quinn.

Gathering her courage, she swung open the door. David waited on the other side. "Hello, Marisol." He leaned forward to kiss her, but she avoided his touch, stepping aside to let him enter. "I'm glad you called. I knew you couldn't stay angry at me forever."

"This isn't a social call," she said. "You're here on business."

"What are you talking about?" David asked.

"I have what you were looking for," she replied. "It arrived by messenger last week."

David chuckled, but there was little humor in the

sound. "So you were lying to me when I was here last?"

"I didn't know what I had until I unwrapped it. The minute I did, I realized that it was the Emory Colter from the Templetons' house. So, is it an original?"

"That depends," he said. "On whether you decided to switch it with the painting in Newport. You see, that's what I was counting on. I suspected your father had sent you the painting. He never had the stomach for my little intrigues. And I knew, once you received it, you'd figure out what you had. And I hoped you'd exchange it for the one in the Templetons' library."

"Because this is the fake," Marisol said.

"Is it?"

She shook her head. "I didn't switch the paintings. See, you don't know me nearly as well as you thought you did." Marisol drew a deep breath, knowing that she'd have to get him to talk more. The agents had pressed her to get as much from him as she could, but questioning him about what he'd done seemed so clumsy. "Why did you do it?"

"Come on, Marisol. The Templetons, and people like them, are the kind of collectors artists hate. They don't collect for the love of art, they collect because it's the fashionable thing to do, a way to keep up with their billionaire friends. They're only interested in how good the investment is. They don't appreciate the beauty of what they've just acquired."

"So that's why you swindle them? Because they deserve it?"

"Well, don't they?"

"Why did you give my father the painting?"

"Because I knew he'd send it to you. And if it was intercepted, I could deny ever knowing anything about it. He makes quite the dupe."

Marisol knew this was the moment when she'd have to keep it together. She'd never been much of an actress, but she tried to imagine how she'd react if Ian hadn't gotten to her first. "How much did you pay him?"

David laughed. "Nothing. He wanted to do it for you. We were engaged and he wanted to give you a beautiful wedding. Of course, any money I made I promised would go back to you. He was silly enough to believe me. But in the end, it didn't make a difference. The painting he gave me was unusable. I had to find someone else to make the copy." He paused. "You know, the funny thing was, he never even noticed. He couldn't tell the difference between what he'd painted and the painting I sent him. Lucky thing or he might not have been so anxious to help me."

Marisol tried to contain her relief. Her father hadn't been involved. He was safe, and in a few moments, she would be safe, too. She pointed to the crate sitting up against the wall. "Take it and get out. I don't ever want to see you again. And if you ever try to contact my father, I'll call the authorities."

He grabbed her arm and pinched it so tightly, Marisol cried out. "Don't threaten me," he warned. With that, he released her, then grabbed the crate and dragged it to the door. "Nice doing business with you, Mari."

When the door shut behind him, Marisol slowly sank to the floor, pulling her knees up to her chest. A shudder raced through her body and she swallowed back a surge of tears. "He's gone," she said, knowing that Ian and the agents were listening.

A few moments later, Agent DiMarco appeared from the rear of the gallery. He helped her to her feet. "You did fine," he said. "You got everything we needed and then some."

"What's next?" she murmured.

"We watch Barnett," DiMarco said. "We wait for him to ship the painting, and then arrest him. He goes to trial, you testify and he goes to jail for a long, long time."

"And my father?"

Agent DiMarco shrugged. "You heard what he said. As far as we're concerned, he had no role in this at all. He's in the clear."

The door to the gallery burst open and Ian strode in, followed closely by Agent Phillips. "Are you all right?" Ian asked.

Marisol nodded. With trembling fingers, she removed the microphone taped to her chest and handed it to Agent Phillips. "Am I finished now?"

Phillips nodded. "We may have a few more questions at a later date, but I think you've done enough for one night. Thank you, Miss Arantes. We'll be in touch. And call us if Barnett makes contact again."

Marisol nodded and watched as the two agents walked out of the gallery.

When they were gone, Ian gathered her in his arms, hugging her fiercely. "When I heard you scream, I nearly jumped out of my skin. I swear, if I ever see Barnett again, he'll be brushing his teeth from the back of his head."

Marisol nuzzled her face into his chest. "Take me to bed," she said. "To your bed. I want to sleep late and then I want to spend the entire day making love and then I want to paint you again."

Ian bent to meet her gaze. "That might have to wait."

"Why?"

"Well, we've got the big firemen's picnic tomorrow and the Fourth of July celebration in town on Monday, and there's a parade I have to lead, a pie-baking contest I have to judge and a bicycle rodeo that I have to supervise. I know it sounds pretty small town for a sophisticated city girl like yourself, but there is a dance tomorrow night."

"I guess I'll have to spend the day alone in bed," she said.

"I was thinking I might need a date for that dance," Ian said, toying distractedly with her hair. "We've been sleeping together for a while now. Maybe we ought to go out on a real date."

Marisol sent him a sideways glance, then smiled. A date sounded good. In truth, a date sounded like the perfect thing for the two of them. But she wasn't quite ready to announce their relationship to the world. "Could we keep things to ourselves for a bit longer?" she asked. "I might need some time to adjust to having a boyfriend."

Ian frowned. "You don't want to go out with me?"

"I do. But all this has happened pretty fast. Don't you think we ought to spend a little more time together before we get all the town gossips buzzing?"

He nodded. "You're probably right."

"But who knows? I might just run into you at the picnic and we could have an ice cream together. Or maybe share a dance? And if you're lucky, I might agree to meet you back at your place later on."

Ian kissed her softly, his tongue damp on her lips. "I think it sounds like a good plan."

Marisol groaned. "No more plans. I've had enough plans for a lifetime. Let's just call it a…start."

Ian nodded. "A beginning." He slipped his arm around her shoulders and they walked to the door of the gallery. When they reached the door, he turned and faced her. "Do you regret that we started in the middle? That we didn't date and get to know each other before we…you know."

Marisol shook her head. She couldn't imagine their relationship beginning any other way except with wild, passionate sex. "If you would have asked me out on a date that first day, I probably would have said no. After David, I was pretty determined to avoid men."

"You would have refused me?" Ian asked, surprised by the revelation.

"Yes. But then, you offered me the one thing I couldn't resist." She ran her fingers down his chest, then grabbed his belt and yanked him against her body.

Ian chuckled. "I guess I have your number, don't I?" he said.

Marisol pushed up on her toes and kissed him playfully. "Yes, you do. And I expect you to use it at least once a day."

His hands circled her waist and he picked her up and wrapped her legs around his hips. "Now there's plan," he said, kissing her neck.

"A very good plan," she murmured.

Epilogue

"WHERE ARE WE GOING?"

Marisol stood at the end of the bed in her apartment over the gallery, fresh from the shower, her naked body wrapped in a towel. She was three days away from the opening of her gallery and Ian had insisted on taking her away from all the work she had to do.

"I'll tell you when we get there," Ian said.

She walked to the closet. "Unless you tell me where we're going, how am I going to know what to wear?"

"Just wear one of those pretty dresses you have. And be sure to wear underwear. Underwear is important."

Marisol turned from the closet and looked at Ian. "Why will I need underwear?"

"Because I don't want to have to be thinking of you not wearing underwear. I want all of that," he said, pointing to her body, "covered."

"Since when have you turned into such a prude?" she asked. "I thought you liked my body. I certainly like yours."

Ian rolled over on the bed, then jumped up and began to rummage through her underwear drawer. He plucked out a black thong and a lacy little scrap that could barely be called a bra. "I can see I'm going to have to buy you some respectable underwear."

Marisol giggled. "And what is respectable underwear? Panties that attend church regularly? Perhaps a bra that does volunteer work at a local hospital?"

"You know what I mean."

She grabbed a dress from the closet, then sat down on the bed next to Ian. "If you want a respectable girlfriend, I don't think I'm the one, Ian Quinn. You know who I am and how I live my life. Without underwear. Why would you want to change me?"

"I just want to change you for today," he said. "Then you can go back to being who you are. I love who you are." He paused, reaching out to caress her cheek. "I love you."

Marisol blinked, the sentiment catching her by surprise. She fought back a surge of emotion as she leaned over and kissed him. He'd never said it out loud, but now he had. And it felt so good to hear it. "I love you, too."

Ian grinned, like a little boy who'd just been handed a key to the candy store. "You do?"

Marisol nodded. "Do you know why I love you? Because you always tell the truth. Now, tell me why I have to wear underwear."

He groaned, grabbing her around the waist. "Because we're going to dinner at my parents' house. Once a month, the whole family gets together for Sunday dinner and I thought it was about time I introduced you to the family."

Stunned, Marisol backed away from Ian. "Today? Did you tell them I was coming?"

"No," he replied. "I thought it could be a surprise. But they won't mind. There's always enough food and room for a guest or two. My sisters bring salads and stuff and my mother cooks a huge feast."

"But I can't go. I don't have anything to wear," Marisol said. "And I don't have any underwear. I can't meet your mother wearing this." She held up the thong. "I mean, what if my skirt blows up…or—I can't."

"You don't have to be nervous," Ian said. "They'll love you. You're talented and funny and you're exactly the kind of girl my brothers and sisters would enjoy."

"How many brothers and sisters?"

"I have four brothers and two sisters and two brothers-in-law and two sisters-in-law. And nine nieces and nephews."

"So, I'll be meeting twenty-one people today, in a shabby dress and obscene underwear?"

Ian took her hand. "I'm the one who should be worried. I made a deal with my brothers that I'd stay away from women for three months. The day after I made the deal, I met you. So much for celibacy."

"Why would you make such a ridiculous deal?" she asked.

"It was like a dare," he said. "And with my brothers, you can't turn down a dare. And there was money involved. The guy who stayed celibate longest got two thousand dollars. And if anyone enjoyed the pleasures of the flesh before the three months were up, they had to pay an extra thousand."

"So you owe two thousand because of me?"

Ian nodded. "But you were worth every penny."

"You didn't even try to resist," she said.

"I know. From the minute I saw you driving that sweet little sports car, I was a goner." Ian grabbed her hand and pulled her down on the bed, pinning her hands above her head. He kissed her softly, running his tongue along her lower lip. "And my family will be goners the minute they meet you."

"Promise?" she asked.

"You are the most important person in my life, Marisol, and it doesn't matter how they feel about you. It won't change my feelings."

"They could hate me," she said.

"I think they'll love you. Now, where is the pretty blue dress you wore the day I met you? Wear that—with underwear, of course."

Marisol reluctantly crawled off the bed and rummaged through her top dresser drawer, frantically searching for her most conservative lingerie. From the bottom of the drawer, she pulled a pair of white cotton bikinis and held them up to Ian. "All right," she murmured. "I can go."

A few minutes later she was dressed and she stood in front of the mirror and rearranged her hair for the last time. Ian walked up behind her and put his hands on her shoulders, then kissed her neck.

"How do I look?"

"You look exactly like the girl I fell in love with." Ian smiled. "Perfect."

Marisol watched him in the reflection of the mirror,

this handsome man who had walked into her world and captured her heart. Someday, maybe she'd be able to understand exactly how two people so determined not to fall in love had done just that. For now, it was enough that they'd found each other. And that they'd love each other forever.

* * * * *

New York Times *bestselling author
Linda Lael Miller is back with a new romance
featuring the heartwarming McKettrick family from
Silhouette Special Edition.*

SIERRA'S HOMECOMING
by Linda Lael Miller

*On sale December 2006,
wherever books are sold.*

Turn the page for a sneak preview!

Soft, smoky music poured into the room.

The next thing she knew, Sierra was in Travis's arms, close against that chest she'd admired earlier, and they were slow dancing.

Why didn't she pull away?

"Relax," he said. His breath was warm in her hair.

She giggled, more nervous than amused. What was the matter with her? She was attracted to Travis, had been from the first, and he was clearly attracted to her. They were both adults. Why not enjoy a little slow dancing in a ranch-house kitchen?

Because slow dancing led to other things. She took a step back and felt the counter flush against her lower back. Travis naturally came with her, since they were holding hands and he had one arm around her waist.

Simple physics.

Then he kissed her.

Physics again—this time, not so simple.

"Yikes," she said, when their mouths parted.

He grinned. "Nobody's ever said that after I kissed them."

She felt the heat and substance of his body pressed against hers. "It's going to happen, isn't it?" she heard herself whisper.

"Yep," Travis answered.

"But not tonight," Sierra said on a sigh.

"Probably not," Travis agreed.

"When, then?"

He chuckled, gave her a slow, nibbling kiss. "Tomorrow morning," he said. "After you drop Liam off at school."

"Isn't that…a little…soon?"

"Not soon enough," Travis answered, his voice husky. "Not nearly soon enough."

USA TODAY bestselling author

BARBARA McCAULEY

continues her award-winning series

SECRETS!

**A NEW BLACKHAWK FAMILY
HAS BEEN DISCOVERED...
AND THE SCANDALS ARE SET TO FLY!**

She touched him once and now
Alaina Blackhawk is certain horse rancher
DJ Bradshaw will be her first lover. But will
the millionaire Texan allow her to leave
once he makes her his own?

Blackhawk's Bond

On sale December 2006 (SD #1766)

Available at your favorite retail outlet.

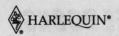

REQUEST YOUR FREE BOOKS!

2 FREE NOVELS PLUS 2 FREE GIFTS!

HARLEQUIN®

Blaze®

Red-hot reads!

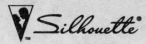

Silhouette®

Romantic
SUSPENSE

From *New York Times*
bestselling author Maggie Shayne

When Selene comes to the aid of an unconscious stranger,
she doesn't expect to be accused of harming him. The
handsome stranger's amnesia doesn't help her cause either.
Determined to find out what really happened to Cory,
the two end up on an intense ride of dangerous pasts
and the search for a ruthless killer.

DANGEROUS LOVER #1443
December 2006

Available wherever you buy books.

INTIMATE MOMENTS™

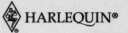

COMING NEXT MONTH

#291 THE MIGHTY QUINNS: DECLAN Kate Hoffmann
The Mighty Quinns, Bk. 3
Security expert Declan Quinn isn't exactly thrilled with his latest job, acting as bodyguard for radio sex-pert Rachel Merrell—until she drags him into her bed and shows him what *other* things he can do to her body while he's guarding it....

#292 SECRET SANTA Janelle Denison, Isabel Sharpe, Jennifer LaBrecque
(A Naughty but Nice Christmas Collection)
Christmas. Whether it's spending sensual nights cuddled up by the fire or experiencing the thrill of being caught under the mistletoe by a secret admirer, *anything* is possible at this time of year. Especially when Santa himself is delivering sexy little secrets....

#293 IT'S A WONDERFULLY SEXY LIFE Hope Tarr
Extreme
Baltimore street cop Mandy Delinski doesn't believe in lust at first sight—at least until she's almost seduced by gorgeous Josh Thornton at a Christmas party. Talk about a holiday miracle! For once it looks as if she's going to get *exactly* what she wants for Christmas—until she finds her "perfect gift" in the morgue the next day....

#294 WITH HIS TOUCH Dawn Atkins
Doing It...Better!
With no notice, Sugar Thompson's business partner Gage Maguire started a seduction campaign...on *her.* That's against all the rules they established years ago. Sure, he's tempting her. Only, it's too bad he seems to want more than the temporary fling she has in mind....

#295 BAD INFLUENCE Kristin Hardy
Sex & the Supper Club II, Bk. 1
Paige Favreau has always taken the safe path. Career, friends, lovers—she's enjoyed them all, but none have rocked her world. Until blues guitarist Zach Reed challenges her to take a walk on the wild side....

#296 A TASTE OF TEMPTATION Carrie Alexander
Lust Potion #9, Bk. 3
After a mysterious lust potion works its sexy magic on her pals, gossip columnist Zoe Aberdeen wants to know the story behind it. When she asks her neighbor—and crime lab scientist—Donovan Shane for help, he's not interested. But thanks to Zoe's "persuasive" personality, he's soon testing the potion and acting out his every fantasy with the sassy redhead....